Praise for

ALL ABOARD,
Destination Unknown

"I have known Virginia Bickel for several years now, and have published several of her short stories in my electronic magazines, *Sonata* magazine for the arts and *Allegro*. Ms Bickel is a fine writer whose forte is stories about the Southwest. Having eagerly looked forward to her novel *All Aboard, Destination Unknown*, I am in no way disappointed. This novel about displaced children is a poignant and well-told picture of children who were taken from their families to live with foster families all over the United States, often never seeing their relatives again. Ms Bickel's novel covers four children from the time they were 'placed out' until their adulthood. It is a job well done, and I highly recommend that you buy *All Aboard, Destination Unknown*, and read this wonderful story."

—Marilyn M. Freeman,
Publisher of *Sonata* magazine for the arts
m.e.stubbs poetry journal
Allegro!

"*All Aboard, Destination Unknown* is a fictional look at an actual event that took place over almost seventy years. It is a view of an event in American history that helped a large number of children find homes during the time of American westward expansion. In a time when parents could die due to disease or working conditions children would be left as orphans to wander the streets and beg their bread. Orphan trains were set up to send these children away from the degradation of the cities to a more wholesome environment in the expanding west of that time; a part of the country we now call the midwest.

"*All Aboard, Destination Unknown* follows four of these children as they leave the streets of a large eastern city and travel west to find new parents and a new life on the farms and in the villages of Illinois, Iowa, and other mid-western states. Even there life was not as rosy as it might have been, but it was far better than what these children had seen before. This is a well-told story of actual events that did occur in our past, and is well worth the reading."

—Robert W. Haseltine
Editor, *USA Magazine*
Author of the novel *Dun Rowans*

ALL ABOARD,

Destination Unkown

JOURNEY TO A NEW LIFE

*Pam,
Enjoy!
Virginia Bickel*

by

Virginia Bickel

*To Presbyterian House
Children & families . . .

Pam Macaulay
2006*

PUBLISH
AMERICA

PublishAmerica
Baltimore

First printing

ISBN: 1-4137-1711-X
PUBLISHED BY PUBLISHAMERICA, LLLP
www.publishamerica.com
Baltimore

Printed in the United States of America

Dedication:

To the memory of my late husband, John W. Bickel; my first born, Illa Bickel Conklin; my first born son, John W. Bickel 11; and my youngest, Perry E. Bickel, and their wonderful families.

Acknowledgements:

I thank Marilyn Freeman for her expert help in editing this manuscript. I deeply appreciate Meredith Muncy's confidence in my ability and her many helpful suggestions. Finally, I thank my friends Joyce Wade and Alfie Geeson for standing by to answer my computer questions.

Chapter One
Leaving New York

A gray sky, laden with clouds sent a cold drizzle down onto Amanda's pinched little face. She would not soon forget this day. With fear in her eyes, the small girl kicked and screamed as Miss Adams pulled her along toward the train platform. Steam billowed out around them as they hurried along. "Come on now," the chaperone chided. "Don't cry; your face will be ugly, all red and smeared with tears."

Amanda cried even louder, "I don't care. I don't care. I don't care. I want to go home to my mamma and papa." She was frightened when she looked at the large, black, monster-looking-thing Miss Adams was pulling her toward. Her eyes burned from the acrid smoke belched forth from the coal burning steam engine of the train. Her hands trembled as she strained, trying to pull away from Miss Adams, struggling for freedom.

Miss Adams pulled her tight against her chest, making a token effort to comfort her. "Hush! You are going to a beautiful place. You will have a new home with new parents and friends. Now stop your sniveling." She thrust a faded blue handkerchief at Amanda. "Here, take this and wipe your nose. I don't want to hear anymore of this nonsense."

Amanda, with a loud sniffle, wiped her nose, tears still trickled from her eyes, staining her cheeks. "I don't want a new home. I don't want new parents." She sobbed again. "I want my mamma and papa." She felt the sting of an open hand slap her face.

"You must stop screaming. You'll frighten the other children and we'll have bedlam. Stay right here." She walked away along the platform to attend other children, leaving the frightened child standing alone.

Amanda immediately started to run away from the train. She felt gentle hands take hold of her shoulders and push her up onto the platform. She heard someone whisper in her ear, "There, there, now don't cry or the old crow will cuff you again." She looked up to see a tall, dark haired boy with jet black eyes looking down at her. "My name is Peter. What is yours?"

"Amanda. Mamma and Papa call me Mandy." He reached into his pocket and took out a round marble-sized ball. "Here, would you like a jawbreaker?"

9

He handed her a piece of hard candy. "Be careful. Don't swallow it. Just let it melt in your mouth; it'll last longer that way."

She took the candy in her hand and slowly put it in her mouth. The biting cinnamon flavor caused her to grimace, but she held it in her cheek as she mumbled, "I don't want to go to a new place. Mamma and Papa won't know where to find me."

"Don't worry about that now." He took her hand and led her to a seat next to a window. "You sit here and you'll be able to see some pretty things when we get out of the city. I heard Miss Adams say we are headed for Texas. Maybe we'll see some cowboys and Indians. Maybe we'll get to ride a pony."

"A merry-go-round?"

"No, I mean real live ponies, the kind that trot over hills and valleys like you see in the movies, not the play-like ones that just go round and round."

Amanda looked puzzled as she swallowed down the juicy liquid produced by the jawbreaker. She didn't know what a movie was, but these words were soothing to her. Still she sobbed and squeezed her eyes shut as hard as she could. She thought, *If I don't look out the window I won't see anything and we won't move. I'll get off this train and run to find Mamma and Papa.* Her heavy wool sweater was damp. Peter took off his worn, hand-me-down coat and covered her shivering body. He was accustomed to helping care for younger children. He patted the top of her head as he had often seen Sister Mary Katherine do when comforting an upset child. "Now don't you worry. You'll be fine." He wished he was more confident that what he said was true.

"You'll get cold without your coat," her voice was barely audible.

"No, silly girl. I'm a boy. Boys are tougher than girls. Don't you know that? Girls are made out of candy and spice and everything nice; boys are made out of hammers and nails, and puppy dog tails. That's what boys are made of." He was trying to say something to make her laugh.

A small smile appeared just for an instant on her swollen little face. "You are a silly boy, Peter."

Peter tried to think of something to say to take her mind off her fears. "I'm eleven years old, practically grown. How old are you, Mandy?"

Still sniffing, Amanda held up seven fingers. Finally she curled her tired little body into a tight ball and crouched under Peter's coat, her eyes still closed, drifted off to sleep. Peter watched her as the train began to move. She kept her eyes tightly closed. *If I don't look out the window the train will stand still and when I open my eyes we will still be here. I'll run off and find my Papa.* The train, one of the last to carry orphans away from the dirty, smoke filled city chugged through the darkness of the summer night; headed south before heading west, carrying forty-five children.

Her dark hair hung in damp ringlets on her collar. Peter could see her shoulders jerk, and hear her soft sobs. *What will I say to make her feel better when she wakes to find that she is a long way from home, and her mamma and papa?*

Miss Adams was careful to see that all the children on the placing out mission were seated in the same car, and as close together as possible, making it easier to keep an eye on them, to see that they behaved as she wished.

As Peter listened to the *puff, puff* of the steam engine he thought about how he came to be on this train with these other children. Some of them came from orphan homes and others taken from detention, having been picked up from the streets of New York City by the police. Others from the Children's Aid Society were placed in a similar program. Peter recognized two others from The Home, Amanda and Jason. *Wonder where the girl sitting beside Jason is from— maybe from one of the other orphanages.*

Just a couple of days before departing on the train, Peter was helping Sister Mary Katherine bring in the laundry. He liked helping with this chore; he liked the fresh smell of the newly dried linens and he liked being near Sister Mary Katherine. She always made him feel warm and loved. They walked down the long corridor carrying baskets of clean clothes when he heard Father O'Gorman call out. "Sister Mary Katherine, I'd like to have a word with you, please." His voice sounded cross to Peter.

Sister Mary Katherine and Peter walked into Father O'Gorman's office. He sat behind a large mahogany desk at the far end of the brightly lit room. Peter stared at the shiny glow of his balding head, fascinated by the oily look. When he opened his mouth, the bright light caught the shimmer of a gold tooth. With a huff and a puff of air, he pushed his heavy body out of the chair. His beady gaze settled on Sister Mary Katherine.

She guessed from his frowning glare that he was about to say something unpleasant. She smiled at Peter. "Now run along, Peter. I'll be with you in a minute."

As Peter walked out of the room he heard the priest say, "Now what is this I hear about you not wanting the boy Peter to be included in the placing out program?" Peter lingered in the hall, standing behind the open door. He wanted to hear what else Father O'Gorman would say, and he wanted most of all to hear Sister's answer. He wished with all his heart that Father Kelly were still here. *This new Priest is not kind like Father Kelly.*

While Peter waited he thought about what the new boy, Jason, told him the day after he arrived at The Home. He boasted that he played on the streets. He said he could take care of himself and didn't need some scarecrow with his collar turned backwards to tell him what to do. He told Peter that the priest in his old parish was mean. "He wore a big gold ring with a large blue stone in it. He was always thumping me on the head with it, saying I would come to no good." He said he overheard the priest say to his father, "Take that boy over to Father O'Gorman. He'll straighten him out, all right.' Me Da begged him not to make me go, but he said it was either that or I would be sent to a place for bad boys; I think he called it a reformatory. Me Da said, 'He's not a bad boy. He stole them apples because he was hungry"

"The old goat said, 'Mind you, do as I say or your boy will end up in jail'. Me Da said, 'I'll take him.'"

Peter remembered the day Jason's father brought him to The Home. He had boxed Jason's ears. "Now you behave yourself and mind the nuns," he told him. Then he grabbed him around the shoulders and gave him an awkward hug. After hearing Jason's story, Peter felt lucky that he had Sister Mary Katherine to watch out for him. He stepped closer to the door. He heard the stern voice of Father O'Gorman. "Sister Mary Katherine, why are you objecting to the boy, Peter, being included in this program? I understand you have always objected when his turn came up to be placed on the Orphan Train?"

Peter peeked through a crack in the door. Sister Mary Katherine held her small body erect; her dark eyes shining with apprehension she answered, "Peter is eleven years old, Father. I fear the only reason a person would adopt him would be for the work he can do. Besides, I need him here. He helps with the smaller children."

Father O'Gorman scowled. "This placing out program has been going on since the mid-1850s. We have placed over 200,000 children. Why are you so opposed to it? These children are sent out west to insure a better life for them. They will experience fresh air and sunshine, have wholesome food, and be cared for by loving parents. That, after all, is the purpose of the program."

"I wish I could be as certain as you are about the loving parents. I beg you not to send Peter away. I say again, he is a great help to me with the smaller children. He helps the other Sisters as well."

"Listen, Sister, these are unfortunate children who, by one circumstance or another, have been left to fend for themselves on the streets of New York or left in orphanages and are wards of the state or church. Some are children of immigrants who, upon landing in America, found they did not have the means to take care of them. Some, of course, are children of unwed mothers."

"I am very much aware of the background of these children, Father. I know most of them find a better life in the rural areas than they would have here, but then there are those others, the ones selected for the work they..."

He interrupted her. "I am not changing my mind, Sister. I'm not as easy to sway as Father Kelly was. It's 1929; we are in the throes of a deep depression. We can't afford to keep all the children that come here. The boy will go. We need the space for other children. Make haste and get him ready. He needs a haircut and some new shoes. Look in the clothes storage closet and find a decent coat and hat for him. Nobody will want to adopt a rag-a-tag kid."

Peter had to listen closely to hear Sister's voice as he peeked through the crack between the door and wall; it now sounded shaky and weak. "Please reconsider, Father."

"I'll hear no more about it, Sister. The boy will go."

There was a long silence. With a sigh of resignation Sister's body slumped forward. Then finally as if with sheer willpower she squared her shoulders and looking at Father O'Garman defiantly; her voice became strong again. "I see little Amanda Polletta is on the list. You can't send her away. I told her father that she would be here when he is able to care for her. I expect him to come for her as soon as he can. You mustn't send her away. I gave my word."

"Now hear this Sister, I can and I will do what I think best for this institution. I will not tolerate insubordination."

He fingered a pile of paper on his desk. "I have her records here in front of me." Her father's last visit was over a month ago. I'm sure we have seen the last of him. The child must go. As I said, we have to make room for other children."

"Father, Mr. Polletta works in a factory twelve hours a day, then comes home to care for his sick wife. He'll come for Amanda when his wife is better or when she meets her reward." Sister Mary Katherine argued to no avail.

Peter hurried away when he heard Sister coming; he stood several feet from the door. He didn't want her to know he heard the conversation between her and Father O"Gorman.

Sister hurried out of Father O'Gorman's office. Her face was taut. Peter had never seen her frown like that before. She gripped his shoulder, "Come along Peter. We'll have a treat in the kitchen." As they drank their cocoa and ate a Danish, Sister Mary Katherine was unusually quiet, thoughtful.

The next morning Sister explained to Peter why he had to go with the other children who were being sent west. "You will have a better life, live with a real family, maybe even have brothers and sisters." Peter knew she was trying to make him feel better about leaving. She again asked him to wait in the hall. "I need to have a word with Father O'Gorman. Like the day before he watched through the crack between the wall and the door. He watched as Sister Mary Katherine marched into Father O'Gorman's office, shoulders squared, voice strong. She scolded, "May I ask why a Placing Agent was not sent ahead of this group of children to choose suitable homes for them as has been done in the past?" She remembered his remark about not allowing insubordination; she didn't care anymore. *Let them send me away to another Parish. It doesn't matter now that Peter will no longer be here.*

He answered her in a plaintive voice. "For one thing there was not enough time, what with Father Kelly leaving suddenly and all. And, anyway, the children from the Children's Aid Society and the detention centers are often sent out without homes being pre-chosen. From what I hear there is no great difference in the success of the two selection methods." He tried to placate her.

"All the same, I worry." He can't do anything to hurt me more than he has already done by sending Peter away. I might as well tell him. "Father Kelly would never have allowed it." She stepped back and waited for his wrath to follow.

"I am not Father Kelly; it would be wise of you to remember that."

Chapter Two
The Trip West

Peter longed for Father Kelly, but he had been sent away for his health. He had developed a bad cough and the doctor recommended that he live in a drier climate out west. *Out west? Maybe I will see Father Kelly. Sister Mary Katherine said this group of children is being sent to Texas. Texas is out west.* His heart felt a little lighter.

Peter was awake long past midnight, as the train rolled bumpily along unsteady tracks. He felt sad when he remembered how Sister Mary Katherine had tears in her eyes when she said good-bye to him yesterday. "Now you be a good boy and always remember to say your prayers." She placed a gold pocket watch in his hand and folded his fingers over it. Taking his fist in both her hands, she said, "This watch belonged to your grandfather. He wanted you to have it. Keep it always and know that he loved you." Before he could ask her who his grandfather was, tears glazed her eyes and she turned and walked hurriedly away. He wondered why he had been placed in The Home if his grandfather loved him. He pondered this question as he sat in the dark car and fingered the smooth stone fob at the end of the gold chain; an activity that would help to alleviate tension from his young body many times in years to come. He wished he knew what his grandfather had looked like; he imagined him as a gray-haired gentleman with a gray beard and bushy brows. In his mind's eye he could see the watch inside his grandfather's vest pocket with the chain hanging loosely across his enormous abdomen, the fob securely resting in the pocket on the other side. That image of his grandfather, as he imagined it, would comfort him in the hard years to come.

The next morning Peter watched Amanda as she squirmed and whimpered while awakening from sleep. She said, "I dreamed that awful thing again. The thing that happened the night before my papa took me to that big house where I first saw you, Peter. I thought I was dreaming when I heard the doctor say to Papa, 'You must send the child away. Maggie is too ill to care for her, and you are away at work all day. Besides, she will surely contract the disease if she stays here in this small room with her mother.'

"At first Papa said, 'No, I can't let her go. It would break Maggie's heart.'

"Then from mamma's bed in the corner I heard her say, 'James, you must do what is best for Amanda. I couldn't stand it if she got tuberculosis from me. Then my heart would break.' Her voice was so weak I could barely hear her.

"Papa looked sad. He said, 'All right, I'll take her to The Home tomorrow.' I held on to Mamma as tight as I could, but Papa pulled me away. Mamma was crying when I left her. My Mamma said I wouldn't have to stay at The Home long. She said Papa would come and get me soon. Now he won't know where to find me."

Amanda realized later that that she was not dreaming that night as she slept on a cot in her Mamma's bedroom. She told Peter, "Now I know it wasn't a dream, but I've dreamed that same dream every night since. The next morning Papa took me to a big, big house. It was real scary, but I was not really afraid because Papa held my hand. He said, 'Now look, Honey, there are swings and seesaws to play on, and other children to play with. Then we went into that big house with lots of windows; it had a big pretty door in the middle. He said I'd be happy there.

"'I won't be happy, Papa,' I told him. 'I don't want to play with other children. I just want to stay with you and Mammy. I have to take care of Mammy.' He didn't answer me."

Amanda said he pulled her along as they walked up many steps and into the largest room she had ever seen. "Sister Mary Katherine was there. She said, 'Don't worry about her Mr. Polletta, we'll take good care of her; keep her safe until you can return for her.'" Amanda began to cry again. "Now Papa can't find me if I am not there."

Peter recalled being there the morning her father brought her to The Home. He'd heard him say, "Be a good girl, Mandy. I'll come for you as soon as I can." He pushed her hair back off her forehead, hugged her, and kissed her cheek. He turned abruptly and walked out the door. Amanda watched as he walked quickly out onto the busy street. She stood looking out the window at him, waving frantically, and crying, "Papa, Papa." He didn't look back.

Peter had also watched when, on those rare occasions, her father came to see her. She stood on his feet, clinging to his legs, and crying to go home with him. He'd say, "You can't go home with me, baby. Your Mamma is sick and can't take care of you while I'm at work." He would pry her fingers loose and push her away. *I could see it broke his heart, but what else could he do?*

The last time he visited her Peter saw that he gave her a gold locket with his picture in one side and her mother's picture in the other. "Sweetheart," he said, his voice cracking. "This was my wedding present to your mother. She asked me to give it to you and tell you that she loves you more than anything in this world." He kissed her sad little face and quickly turned away so she would not see his eyes glossed over with tears. *He must have known her mother was near death and that she would not see her beloved little girl again.*

The rhythm of the train rocking lulled Peter into a restless sleep. He was awakened with a start by Amanda's scream. "No, no, I won't get *buckleosis*! I won't, I won't!" Her eyes opened wide with horror as she realized that it was only a dream. He had an idea. He reached across Amanda and drew a funny face on the foggy train window. "Look, Mandy, this is a clown. He's smiling at you. He wants you to smile back at him." She did. "Would you like me to tell you a story about a clown?"

"Yes, tell me a story, Peter."

Peter thought hard. *What story can I tell Mandy about a clown that will have a happy ending?* He told her the story about the happy toy clown that jumped up and down on *The Little Engine That Could*, helping it get over the mountain. Then he told her about *Sleeping Beauty*, and many other stories, while the train rumbled across the countryside. The next day when they saw a burro in a field he told her about the donkey that thought he was a lap dog and tried to sit on his master's lap. She laughed at that one. When they saw chickens along the way, he told her about the chicken that thought the sky was falling. A rabbit in the meadow reminded him to tell her about the rabbit that wanted red wings; a pig prompted the story about the three little pigs.

In the seat behind Peter sat a girl whose fair skin, blue eyes and blonde hair were in marked contrast to Peter and Amanda's dark Italian coloring. Laura was twelve. She listened intently to Peter's stories. Some of them she remembered her grandfather telling her. It made her sad to think of him. He was so brave as his frail body lay ravaged by that awful flu. She remembered his exact words. "I'm sorry, my dear Laura, I may have to leave you. I arranged for a relative to come over from Germany to run the store and take care of you. You be a good, brave girl, and I'll see you in heaven someday." She gave her promise, and she would keep it. She thought, *I will be good and I will be brave. I did not cry—not even when that awful man, Ralph, came and said he was Grosspapa's nephew, and said the store was his now. Not even when the very next day after Grosspapa was buried he called the Children's Aid Society and told them to come for me.*

I did not cry. Not even when they said they had no room for me, and that since I am Catholic I might be happier with the nuns, and then brought me here to this train, I did not cry.

Laura sat with head bent forward, hands over her face. *I wish I could have said goodbye to Ma and Pa Strassberger before Ralph sent me away. They were Grosspapa's best friends. They'll wonder where I am, why I don't come to the restaurant to get kuchen for teatime like I did when Grosspapa was there. It makes me sad, but I will not cry.*

Jason tapped Laura on the shoulder. "What's the matter with you—you bawling?" He asked in a voice that sounded deeper than expected of a boy; more like that of a young man. She looked up to see a sturdily built boy of about her own age. His straight, stubby hair looked like a thatch of wheat. He was looking curiously at her with hazel colored eyes.

Laura just looked at him. "I am not crying."

"Well, you're simpering then. It won't do you no good here. Might as well buck up and spit in their eye for all the good it'll do you." He bragged, "I don't worry. I can take care of myself—whatever comes my way I can handle it, just like that." He snapped his finger.

Laura recognized him as the boy named Jason who had been pacing up and down the isle. He swaggered by several times whistling a tune she didn't recognize. As he neared where Peter and Amanda sat he started to tease, sing-songing, *"Ya, ya, ya, ya, ya, Peter plays with girls, Peter plays with girls."* But Laura saw that he always managed to sit close by so he could hear the stories Peter told Amanda. Laura thought she understood Jason. *He's just trying not to think about what might lay ahead for him*

Jason plopped down in the seat next to Laura. "Where did you come from? I don't remember seeing you in that home where me and Peter wuz."

"No I was sent to the train this morning from the Children's Aid Society. They said they didn't have room to keep me, and they said I'd feel more at home with this group anyway since I'm Catholic. Did you know Peter at The Home?"

"Sort of. He was always hanging around, helping one of the nuns. Reg'lar sissy if you ask me."

"I think he seems nice."

Jason stood up. "Hurmph. I don't like anything about any of this stuff. Just let anybody try to boss me, I'll show them. But I recken anything will be better than being in that home with that fat ass O'Gorman. I'll just set here if you don't mind, and listen to them sissy stories Peter's is telling that silly little girl."

18

Chapter Three
The Placing Out

When the train stopped in Texarkana, Texas, the school band came out to meet them. The Mayor was effusive in his welcoming speech. He stood on the train platform in his white shirtsleeve, no coat or tie. His sparse hair fluttered in the wind. His plump pale hand reached out from his rotund body to touch each child as they stepped off the train. After all the children had alighted he stepped back a few paces. "I want all you children to know that we are happy to have you stop in our town, and we'll love having some of you stay here with us permanently." By the time he finished speaking the children were beginning to fidget. "Now we want all you children to follow me about two blocks to the Saint Agnes Church; we goin' to have a party to celebrate you bein' here. Y'all come on now." He led them to the church basement where they had refreshments. There were balloons for everybody. By the time the train was serviced, and the placing out was finished, they were ready to be on their way. Fourteen selections were made.

Peter wondered if he had been wrong in telling his friends, Laura and Mandy, how to act to keep from being chosen. Twenty-one of the children were still aboard when they left Texarkana. The following morning the train chugged on through the flat, sandy land of East Texas where they saw tomatoes and other vegetable crops growing in the fields.

As they went further west the terrain changed from pine trees and sandy soil to oak trees and black land where they saw fields of cotton so white it looked as if the plants were daubed with snow. Before their stop in Clarksville, Texas, seventy-five miles west of Texarkana, they were given lunch of the usual ham and egg sandwich, an apple and a glass of milk. Miss Adams cautioned with a stern face, "Get washed up and dressed. And I don't want to see any more of your antics: squirming and scratching and frowning." Upon arrival they were marched from the train depot to the town square, where they stood in the shadow of a statue of a Confederate soldier. There they were to be inspected by the prospective parents.

Peter told Amanda, "Don't forget, put your finger in your mouth, hold your head down and scream as loud as you can."

"Why, Peter?"

"Nobody will choose you if they think you are a screamer and the further we go there will be fewer children to choose from, and the more likely we are to be chosen in the same town, maybe even by the same people."

"Oh, goodie. I'll cry real loud, Peter. You'll see."

Jason did his usual scowl as he looked out over the crowd. *If they don't like the looks of me they'll choose another kid, not me. Then at the end of the line I'll run off and they won't see me no more. I'll join a gang of outlaws; maybe a gang like the James brothers.* The ploy worked, he wasn't chosen even though it was a cotton farming community and many of the larger, stronger looking boys were taken, no doubt for the work they could do in the fields. Ten more children left the train, leaving only eleven.

The whole affair was unceremoniously over in an hour.

Peter was happy not to be chosen. He wanted to go further west: west to real cow country. Besides, the further he west went the more likely he was to find Father Kelly.

Another day and night was spent on the train before it stopped again except to take on water and fuel. They traveled through wooded areas and as they went further west they began to see sandy soil again. Mesquite and tumbleweeds dotted the area. Amanda was fascinated when she saw a long legged bird running along side the train. "Look, look, Peter. What is that? Is that a chicken?

"No, I read about that bird. It's a chaparral. People out here call it a road runner."

"Why, Peter?"

"Because it can run so fast. See, it's almost keeping up with the train."

The windmills were another fascination for Amanda. She thought Peter knew the answer to all questions. "Look Peter, there's a big fan in the field. It's going round and round? It's keeping the cows cool."

"I don't know what that is, Amanda, but I'm sure it is not a fan." That was one thing Sister had not told him about and he had not read about it in a book. "I'll find out what it is as soon as I see Miss Adams," he told her.

At last the day came when the Train Children were to be presented for adoption in Weldon, Texas. They were given the same cold sandwich of salty cured ham and an egg, an apple and a glass of milk. It made Peter very thirsty and he was beginning to tire of this fare. "Maybe we should try to get chosen here," he told Amanda. "Aren't you getting tired of this train, Mandy? Put on your best smile, and maybe someone here will want us. We are out west now." He gave the same advice to Laura and Jason.

"I don't want to get chosen," Jason said.

Before the train stopped each child was cleaned up, hair was combed, and clean, new clothes provided. Miss Adams admonished them firmly. "Now you children listen to me. I want you to walk out on that platform, wave to the people and smile. Everyone likes a happy child. Amanda, keep your finger out of your mouth and no more of that screaming. Laura, straighten up those shoulders and try to walk like a lady. And Jason, I don't want to see you frowning and grimacing out there."

Jason thought, but did not speak it aloud, *Oh yeah, if you don't want to see me grimacing out there you better not watch me.*

Peter wasn't reprimanded. At the other stops he had been clever and waited until he was out of Miss Adams's sight before he started to limp. Outside the train window he saw a crowd of people waiting on the platform. They looked strange to him. Some of the men wore large hats; they looked like the cowboys he had seen in a Bob Steele western movie; it was called a talkie, the first he ever saw. The women wore long, dark, dresses; most of them made of cotton. Some wore bonnets that covered most of their face. Others were well dressed and wore hats decorated with feathers or flowers. He heard a man say as he walked down the isle, "I guess the flapper style hasn't reached this far west."

The children were herded onto the platform and instructed to follow Miss Adams. This time they were taken to the Knights of Columbus hall and told to walk up onto the stage and stand there until they were called. The selection process began. They were chosen one by one, then led away to a makeshift desk near the entrance to the large room. Mrs. Waters, a middle-aged woman wearing an ostrich feather in her large hat waited there to record the necessary information.

Laura was placed on the front row. Her dress hung below her coat. She pulled at the garters that held up her black cotton stockings. Try as she would, she could not smile. As she stooped to tie the string of one of her scuffed shoes, she heard a voice say, "I would like the girl on the left; the blonde one with the buster brown hair cut." Laura winced at hearing the shrill voice. She looked up to see a woman who appeared to be in her mid-thirties pointing at her. Her chestnut brown hair was pulled back in a large bun that showed from under the flower-bedecked brim of the large rose-colored hat she wore; she carried a parasol of the same color. Her lighter rose-colored taffeta dress was trimmed with ecru lace, and billowed out from a cinched waist. "Come along girl, I'm Mrs. Pucket," she said, as she led Laura to the makeshift desk.

Mrs. Waters, the local coordinator, smiled as she addressed Laura. She confirmed the information that had already been given to her on the list of children. "What is your name, young lady? What is your age, your date of birth, the name of your parents; are they living?"

After they finished the necessary paperwork Laura followed along behind the woman, carrying the case that held her meager belongings. They walked several blocks to Mrs. Pucket's house. It was a large white house; it had a wraparound porch and dark green shutters and gingerbread trim. Grayish-green bushes with small purple flowers grew around the circular porch. In the yard a sign read, *Room and Meals, Reasonable.*

Jason's turn to be chosen came. "Hello, son. My name is Sam Woolridge. We would like to have you join our family. How do you feel about that?"

"Fine, Sir," Jason was on his best behavior. *I might as well get it over with. I'll shuck them soon enough once I get away from this train.* Together they walked to a Model A Ford. In the car was a lady with auburn hair, and eyes the same russet color as Jasons's.

"Grace, this is Jason. Aren't we lucky? We got the boy you wanted; the one with the red hair."

"Thank you, Sam." Reaching up, she gave her husband a kiss on the cheek. Then she put her arm around Jason and gave him a motherly squeeze. She smiled at her husband and asked, "What do you think Mary Anne will think of her new brother?"

"She'll love him."

Yeah, I'll bet.

"Son, would you mind riding in the rumble-seat. We don't have far to go."

Rumble seat, huh? I've heard of them, but this is the first time I've seen one of them things. Good, I won't have to talk to them.

Several other children were chosen. The same procedure was followed. First they went by the desk where Mrs. Waters took their name and other information, and the name of the person by whom they were chosen. As they walked away with their prospective parents most of them turned and waved to the children left behind.

Finally, a middle-aged couple took Amanda away. She wiped at tears that flowed with her little fists, smearing them all over her face, causing the dark ringlets to stick to her cheeks. She turned and looked wistfully at Peter, and called out, "Peter, Peter!" as she was led toward a waiting car. Pulling her hand out of the man's large fist that held her tight, she started running toward Peter. "Wait, wait! I want to stay with you."

The man ran after her, his wife close behind, he begged, "Come back little one. We chose you because we have always wanted a little girl just like you. My name's Elmer, and this is my wife, Marie. We want to be your Mommy and Papa and take care of you."

"I have a Mammy and Papa already," Amanda yelled.

Marie tried to hug her, but Amanda pulled away and ran to Peter. He took her hand and squeezed it tight. Looking up he saw two kind faces looking down at Amanda. "Mandy, you can't stay with me. These nice people want you to go home with them. Don't worry, you'll be fine."

Amanda looked woefully at Peter, then turned dejectedly and let Marie take her hand. Sobs were still shaking her little body when Peter last saw her. Lowering his head, he turned and walked slowly back to his place in line.

He watched as Laura and Jason were led away. Sad and half-sick, he wondered if he'd ever see his friends again.

From far back in the crowd Clem Scroggins, a large, ruddy-faced man raised his hand. The wide brim of his Stetson hat was curled up on each side, and the band showed a wide perspiration mark from under the band where it fit around his head. "I'll take this young man," he said, as he walked forward, up the steps of the stage, gruffly placing his hand on Peter's shoulder. He was disgruntled because Sam Woolridge had taken that robust-looking chap with red hair. He would have preferred him; he looked much stronger than this Peter. "I'll just have to make do with what's left," he grunted loud enough for Peter to hear him as they walked away.

Peter gave him a doubtful look, but turned and walked down the steps behind him. They stopped at the desk to answer the questions. Mrs. Waters had been informed which of the children didn't know the names of their parents, thus saving such children the embarrassment of answering that question. *I'm lucky Sister Mary Katherine knew my last name. How did she know? My grandfather must have told her.* He hadn't thought to wonder about that before.

Clem Scroggins' wife, a small, pretty, pleasant looking woman, sat on the spring-seat of a waiting wagon. She was dressed in a calico dress and a bonnet of the same fabric in the style worn by most farmwomen of the time. The crown was gathered onto a stiffly starched brim and a flap hung down in back to protect her neck from the sun. "This here's my wife, Annie. We live on a farm about six miles west of here. It's a long trip by wagon. We best get goin'."

Annie looked hesitantly at her husband. "I hope you will be happy with us, Peter. Here, I brought that pillow for you to sit on. Are you thirsty?" She handed him a quart fruit jar that she had kept wrapped in a wet dishtowel to keep cool. Peter was thirsty, but the water had a strange taste. He would later find it was Gypsum water pumped from the deep wells by the windmills he and Amanda had seen turning in the pastures earlier.

"Thank you, ma'am." *Mrs. Scroggins seems nice, but Mr. Scroggins seems a little gruff; reminds me of Father O'Gorman.*

"Getti-up Red, getti-up Nell. Let's go home," Mr. Scroggins called to the pair of small, red, perfectly matched mules. He slapped the sides of their backs with the flat leather reins.

Chapter Four

Settling In

Laura was agog as Mrs. Pucket led her through the nicely furnished parlor. She had never seen a room like that. A thick Oriental rug covered a shiny hardwood floor. She knew about oriental rugs because Ma Strassberger had one very much like this one. A plush maroon-colored sofa sat across one corner of the room, a floor lamp with an ivory colored shade fringed with maroon to match the sofa stood behind it. Dark green damask draperies hung at the windows, and large old pictures of well-dressed, stern-faced people looked down from the wall.

Mr. Pucket uttered haughtily, "Your room is upstairs and to the back. Follow me." In contrast to the rest of the house, the room was small and sparsely furnished with a bed, dresser, small desk, and straight-backed chair. A curtain made of a bed sheet and gathered on a wire was fastened across one corner. "You can hang your coat and anything else you want to hang on the hooks behind the curtain," Mrs. Pucket said.

"Thank you ma'am. This is a very nice room." It was clean and bright, nicer than Laura was accustomed to in her room above Grosspapa's store. The yellow bedspread and curtains gave it a sunny, cheerful look.

"When you've put your things away come on downstairs and get washed up. It's time to set the table for lunch."

"Yes Ma'am." She was tired but she must be a good girl, and do as she was told as she had promised Grosspapa."

She seems to have good manners and a good attitude, Mrs. Pucket thought. *However, I mustn't get emotional about this girl. I must remember my reason for asking for her. There is so much to be done around here.*

Just as they reached the bottom of the stairs the front door opened to admit a tall, swarthy-complexioned man of medium build. His rumpled clothes, though fine cut, along with his unkempt hair and stubby beard added to his disheveled appearance. He reeled as he stumbled toward Laura, catching hold of her shoulder to steady himself. "Well, hello. Whash thish pretty girl doing here?"

Startled, Laura shrank back from him, but managed to say, "How do you do, sir?"

Mrs. Pucket gave him a stern look and spoke sharply. "Roy, this is Laura, the girl I spoke of asking for at the placing out. Now, please go upstairs and lie down. I'll being some hot coffee up soon. Go on."

"Okay, pretty lady, if you shay sho."

Holding onto the banister he made his way up the stairs.

No explanation was forthcoming from Mrs. Pucket.

By the time the Scroggins pulled into the sandy, rocky yard of their home the sun was a large orange-colored ball starting to set behind a purplish cloud. The house stood on a barren hill overlooking a deep valley to the west. The barn and silo dwarfed the unpretentious whitewashed clapboard house. A porch across the front extended from one side to the other; in the middle was a wide hall, called a dog run.

"Your room is upstairs and to the right, boy." Clem Scroggins scowled. Peter picked up his Gladstone bag Sister Mary Katherine packed his clothes in and followed Mrs. Scroggins up the narrow stairway. She opened a door and ushered him into a spotlessly clean room. It was scantily furnished with a dresser, a shelf that could be used for a desk, and a slat-backed chair. The bed was covered with a quilt made of brightly colored squares; each square tacked in the middle with red wool yarn. On one wall hung a pine rack with five pegs to be used for hanging clothes.

"Just put your case here by the door, son," Mrs. Scroggins said as she lit the coal oil lamp that occupied a corner of the dresser. "Then come on down to the kitchen and wash up. There'll be time for unpacking later. I'll heat up the stew I cooked this morning for our supper. I hope you like apple pie. I baked one in honor of our first meal together."

"Thank you," Peter said. "It's my favorite." *That stew warming on the stove smells good, and I can't wait to taste that apple pie with the cinnamon in it.*

Peter thought about his friends, especially Amanda, Jason, and Laura. *I wonder where my friends are. I hope I get to see them soon.*

Morning came early for Peter. A rooster crowed announcing a new day. Peter had not heard a rooster crow before, but recognized the sound immediately. Sister Mary Katherine had often told him the story of Chanticler, the proud rooster whose fate was sealed when he closed his eyes and crowed once too often, enabling the clever fox to catch him. Peter stretched and yawned. He was thinking about the happenings of the past few days when he heard a loud rap on the door. "Jar the floor in there boy, we got work to do." "Jar the floor"—he would learn to dread the sound of those words.

Peter dressed quickly and ran downstairs. He was met by Mrs. Scroggins. "Come, dear. Sit down and eat your breakfast."

He enjoyed a meal of sausage, eggs, gravy, and biscuits. He thought it much better than the oatmeal and toast he was accustomed to having at The Home.

Soon after he finished eating Mr. Scroggins said, "Come boy, let's get at the chores. There's milking to be done before you go to school. They don't bring milk in bottles out here." Peter was concerned. The only cows he had ever seen were the ones out the train window.

Peter heard a loud noise; looking around he saw the back screen-door slam shut. A thin, middle-aged man came in carrying an armful of wood. He piled it in a box behind the range. "From here on that will be your job, boy." Mr. Scroggins informed Peter. "Jeff's got other work to do."

Jason's first day with his new family was quite different from Peter's. A few miles east, in Weldon, Jason sat at the breakfast table with his new family. *What is the catch here? These people ain't bein' nice for nuthin. They didn't even get cross when I spilled me milk. I know they saw me tip me glass over on purpose. Me Da wouda give me the back o' his hand; so would Father O'Gorman. And that prissy little Mary Anne is constantly watching me. I thought her eyes would bug out of her head when she saw me sop up me gravy with me biscuit. I put the whole thing in me mouth; even that didn't get a cross word from them. Makes me wonder what they are up to.*

Marie and Elmer Brown, Amanda's new parents, were thrilled to bring this lovely little girl into their home. They sat long into the night talking, wondering what to say to Amanda to relieve her pain or at least to render it less severe. "Poor child," Elmer said. "She continues to want her parents. I don't know how to tell her they are dead."

Elmer and Marie walked into the cheerful little nursery they had prepared for Amanda when they saw the article in the paper stating that the Orphan Train would stop in Weldon. Everything was blue and white with a touch of red. They had anticipated coming home with a little boy, but when they saw the beautiful, sad-faced little girl they forgot all about wanting a boy and asked for her. They looked at her in the dim light from the night-lamp on top of the white

27

chest of drawers. Her face was tear stained and her little body shook with sighs from spent sobs.

Marie whispered her concerns. "She insists her father is coming for her. We must be patient. God will show us the way."

"In the meantime her little heart is breaking. I just wish I knew some way to make her feel better. I wish they would give us more information about her, about why she was in an orphan home to begin with. What happened to her parents? We would know better how to deal with her."

In hushed tones Elmer answered, "She keeps asking for the boy Peter; the one she was holding onto at the train station. I have to find him." They quietly closed the door and walked slowly into their room to spend a night of disturbed sleep.

When Amanda awoke during the night she longed for the cot in the corner of her parent's shabby room. In her anxiety she cried out for Peter. Marie ran into the room, and stood by her bed patting her shoulder. "There, there, Mandy, everything will be all right." When she opened her eyes later during the long night, she found Marie sitting in a rocking chair beside her bed.

In the early light of morning Amanda looked around at the cozy room. She saw that stuffed toys surrounded her. Clowns danced on the window curtains and bed coverlet. A teddy bear sat on a small stool near her bed. *I must be in a toy store.* Then she remembered the train and the man and woman who said they were her new mamma and papa. *They don't understand; I have my own mamma and papa.*

When daylight came Elmer walked into her room. He patted her hand. "Good morning, Merry Sunshine. How is our little one this bright sunny day? We have waited so long for a little girl like you."

"I'm not your little girl. I want Mamma and Papa. And I want to see Peter."

Elmer didn't know what to say. Thinking her parents dead he thought, *I can't tell her now that her parents are dead, I just can't.* "Who is Peter? Is he your brother?"

"He's my friend. He tells me stories. He was on the train."

"What is Peter's last name?"

She wiped big tears from her eyes with the back of her hands. "I don't know. He's just Peter. Can I see him?"

"I'll try to find him, little one." Elmer had no idea who took Peter. He sought to change the subject. "We'll talk about it later. In the meantime, uppie, uppie." He lifted her from the bed. "Let's see what Mom Marie has fixed for our breakfast."

She started sobbing again. "Mamma is at home. She's sick; she can't fix breakfast. My papa fixes my breakfast."

Elmer carried her downstairs and seated her at the breakfast table.

Trying to think of something to cheer Amanda, Marie asked her, "How would you like to go for a walk after breakfast? A little boy down the street has a new puppy."

Amanda didn't answer. She was quiet and withdrawn. She ate a few bites of oatmeal and fingered the toast before asking to be excused. "Her manners are good; you can tell she has had proper raising." Marie's heart went out to this little lost child.

Breakfast finished, Elmer set out to find Peter. First he went to the train station where he was told that the train had pulled out at midnight the night before, going further west to other towns where it was hoped the rest of the children would find homes. There was no chance to talk to Miss Adams. He also learned that Mrs. Waters, the coordinator, was not available. She and her husband left on an early morning bus, headed for California to be to be with her sick mother. She was not expected to return for some time. Where, then, they wondered, could they turn?

Chapter Five

School Starts

Two weeks after arriving in Weldon, Peter looked forward to that first day of school. As he put the last bite of hot buttered biscuit in his mouth and drained the last drop of milk from his glass he saw Mrs. Scroggins look up from wrapping sausage and biscuits in newspaper. She spoke to the hired hand. "Jeff, harness up Chock and bring my buggy around to the front. I'm taking Peter to school, it being his first day and all."

Her husband grumbled, "You'll spoil the kid, just like before." Mrs. Scroggins lowered her head and looked for a minute like she might cry. Peter wondered what he meant. Had they taken an orphan before? If so, where was he now? Had he died? He put on the plaid lumberjacket and corduroy cap that the Scroggins gave him, and followed Mr. Scroggins out to the large weathered barn. It had stables on both sides of a wide-open space that was open at both ends. A ladder at the far end of the opening reached up to a loft on which hay and sacks of oats were stored. Pointing to the ladder Mr. Scroggins said, "Climb up there, boy, and throw down a bail of hay. Peter found the bail heavy, but managed to tumble it down. Mr. Sroggins took a pitchfork from a rack on the wall and handed it to Peter. "Come on down here and throw hay into each of these stables for the mules and cows to eat."

Everything was strange to Peter. He wished he could talk to Sister Mary Katherine.

After chores were finished Peter climbed onto the seat of Mrs. Scroggins' buggy. He admired the sleek dark red horse. The white jagged mark on Chock's forehead looked like a streak of lightning, white against a dark sky, and his flowing honey colored tail reminded him of a waterfall they passed while riding the train from New York. Mrs. Scroggins was an excellent driver; Chock seemed to understand what her every movement of the reins wanted him to do. She asked him about his ride on the train; was it comfortable, was the food good, and did he get to know the other children that rode with him.

As they neared the schoolhouse Peter saw that it was a long, white building with two entrances on the front. On one end was painted in large, black, block letters, LANE'S HILL SCHOOL, DISTRICT 15. After about twenty minutes she halted Chock in front of the schoolhouse by pulling gently on the reins. "Whoa Chock." Turning to Peter she patted his shoulder. "I'll come for you when school is out this afternoon."

"I could walk, ma'am. I know the way now."

"I would rather come for you this first day." She bid him bye, turned the horse and buggy around and was gone.

Being accustomed to crowded conditions in the city, Peter was bewildered by the wide-open spaces, but squared his shoulders and looked around at the countryside. The two-room country school was located on a high hill. The school ground was covered with sand and rocks. Longhorn cattle grazed among the scrawny Mesquite in the valley below. In the distance a windmill whirred, bringing forth the water that sustained life for livestock on the arid land.

At eight o'clock the principal stood on the stoop outside the door of the *big room*, and rang a bell; it was called the big room because that was where the higher grades were taught. The children in grades six through eight lined up in front of that entrance; their place in line designated by the seat they occupied in the schoolroom. The children in the lower grades lined up in front of the other door where their teacher stood. Some of the boys were playing around, punching each other, and laughing. The teacher's face took on a severe look as she said to them, "You will stand there until you can behave yourselves." After they settled down she said, "You may march in and take your seats; be quiet about it."

"My name is Mrs. Langford, Peter. Do you want to tell us a little about yourself?"

"Yes ma'am. I'm from New York City."

This brought a snicker from some of the boys.

Mrs. Langford was a stout lady with black hair and milky white skin. When she spoke she was annoyed with the students' bad behavior; her dark eyes flashed. She scolded, "You boys behave yourselves. You know what I mean when I say, sit on yourselves or I'll sit on you."

At recess time Peter noticed that there were two water fountains, one in each room. The water came from an elevated tank located in back of the building. It was fed from a windmill at the edge of the schoolyard. The children were expected to satisfy their thirst, and use the outside toilet during recess. If the need arose during class-time they could raise their hand and ask to be excused. Many times Mrs. Langford, suspecting boredom, rather than nature

31

calling, denied the request.

His first day was uneventful except for the few snickers when he said he was from New York City. He didn't see anything funny about that. He guessed they were thinking about him being a Train Kid. He ignored the rudeness and took his notebook and pencil from his book satchel.

In Weldon, a few miles east of the Scroggins farm Jason sat at the breakfast table with his new family. The sun was shining and a cool breeze ruffled the bottom half of the cottage curtains. *I'm still wonderin' what is the catch here? I know these people ain't bein nice for nothin. I can't believe my ears.* Mr. Woolridge mopped up the milk I spilled again. "Don't worry son; no harm done. Finish your breakfast and get ready for school. I'll give you a ride in my new flivver."

"School? I don't go to school. Me Da said I didn't need to go no more. I can write me name and do figers. I can read some too."

"Well, son, winter is coming on and these days can get pretty long if you have nothing to do but sit here and listen to the wind howl and watch the tumbleweeds blow across the prairie. Just give it a try for a few days? You may find you like it."

"I'll try it jest today." *I'll fool 'em. I'll go along until I figer out what's going on.*

"Fair enough. Here's your book satchel; it contains all the supplies you'll need for now: tablet, pencil, pen staff, ink, ruler and crayons."

"Crayons? I ain't no baby. I'm eleven years old. Me Da says I'm near growed up."

"I understand; just leave them in there for now. You might want to color a map or something." Sam Woolridge could see that this boy would be a challenge, but he figured he was up to it. Grace would be heartbroken if they had to let him go. Already he could see a worried look on her face as she went about her morning chores.

Mr. Woolrige dropped Jason off at the Weldon Elementary School just after the bell rang for morning classes to begin. "Come in, Jason, and sit in that empty seat on the back row," Miss Pearl said. She had met with the Woolriges the day before and knew to expect Jason.

He started to walk hesitantly back to the seat the teacher pointed out. Halfway there a foot clad in a cowboy boot tripped him. He got to his feet and drew back his fist, but Miss Pearl rushed down the isle and grabbed his arm and held it firmly, all the time staring at the culprit. "I'll see you after school,

Vernon Morgan. Take your seat, Jason."

"I'll get you," Jason muttered in the ear of the perpetrator while leaning over pretending to tie his shoe.

Raising from a stooped position, he proceeded to his assigned seat. He was still seething with anger when the boy seated in front of him turned to look at him and whispered loud enough so those around him could hear, "Train Boy." Jason controlled his urge to hit him. *I'll get that kid later, too.*

Fortunately Sam Woolride was waiting for him when the last bell rang. *No chance today, but I'll get'em yet.*

Elmer sought to draw him out about how his day went. "How did it go, son? Make any new friends?"

Jason let out an explosion of pent up anger. "I ain't goin' there no more. Them kids think they are smart. They threw paper wads at me and called me 'Train Boy'. Besides, the teacher put me in with little kids. Makes me feel plum silly. I oughta be in fifth grade with Laura, not in fourth grade with them dumb babies. I ain't goin' back."

Mr. Woolrige thought it best to let it go for now. "There's a Western movie on at the Avalon; it's the first talkie to be shown in town. Marie and I thought you and Mary Ann might like to see it. What do you say?"

"I guess so."

The following morning at breakfast Mr. Woolrige, choosing to ignore Jason's declaration that he would not go back to school matter-of-factly said, "Finish your breakfast, Jason, and get ready for school. I'll give you a ride on my way to work."

"School? I ain't goin' there today or any other day. Them kids think they're smart. They made fun of me. My name ain't 'Train Boy', it's Jason."

"Jason, Miss Adams told me that you are a bright boy, and that all you need is a chance to go to school. Not that I needed her to tell me that. I can see it for myself. Don't you want to show those boys that you are as smart as they are, maybe smarter."

"I already know me numbers bettern' them."

"Before long you'll be reading and writing and spelling as well as they do too, maybe even better."

The long talk the Woolridges had with him finally convinced him that he should go back and show those kids that he was not a dummy.

"I think sending Mandy to the Lutheran Kindergarten is the right decision," Elmer told Marie. "Especially since she has not attended school before, and considering the trauma she has been through. The Reverend Taylor said he'd keep a watchful eye on her."

"Shh," Marie cautioned. "She's coming downstairs."

"Good morning Merry Sunshine." Elmer put Amanda's little red sweater over her dark blue gingham dress. "Now there you go. You could pass for Little Bo Peep."

"Can I have a little lamb?"

"I don't know why not. Now run along with Mamma Marie and be a good girl."

Ah, she is already learning how to play Elmer. Marie had to smile.

Marie pretended not to notice when Amanda pulled back when she took her hand to lead her into the school building. "Miss Hulen, this is our little girl, Amanda; we call her Mandy." She came to us from New York City. Aren't we lucky to have her come to live with us?"

Miss Hulen, knowing the situation, took particular notice, squatting down eye-level with Amanda she took her small hands in hers. "I say you are lucky. Mandy, we are so happy to have you with us." Amanda stood silently, looking down at her high-top shoes.

"Bye, Mandy, I'll come back for you at noon. After lunch we'll go to the drug store and have a nice big bowl of your favorite ice cream." Marie turned to go, leaving Amanda gazing after her, tears lodged in her lashes, with two fingers thrust in her mouth.

Mrs. Pucket walked into the kitchen. "Laura, leave the rest of the breakfast dishes and get dressed. You are expected to attend school. That is part of the pledge I made when I applied for a Train Child. I want you to be there on time, but there will be chores to do when you get home, so don't tarry when you get out.

"Yes Ma'am." She rushed up stairs and dressed in the new red plaid skirt and white blouse Mrs. Pucket bought for her. She placed a narrow black ribbon under her collar and tied it in a bow at her throat. *There, that looks nice.* She whisked a brush through her straight, blonde hair and hurried down stairs. Calling bye to Mrs. Pucket before closing the door behind her.

Laura walked the seven blocks to school. Everything seemed strange. There were no tall buildings, no clutter in the streets or shabbily dressed children begging for food. She looked up and down the main street on which she walked; she looked as far as her eyes could see. She was fascinated to see tumbleweeds rolling across the street in front of her. *I wish I could tell*

Grosspapa about this place, she mused as she walked along swinging her new book satchel. She was happy to be starting to school.

Peter found his studies easy. Mrs. Langford soon discovered that he was a bright boy and that the work in fifth grade was no challenge for him.

Shortly after school started, Mr. Fisher called him aside. "Peter, come in here for a minute, please. I'd like a word with you."

Peter was puzzled. Mr. Fisher walked into his room followed by Peter. He sat down at his desk, and indicating the chair at the end of his desk. "Take a seat there, Peter." Clearing his throat, he said, "Mrs. Langford tells me you are doing very well, that you have already covered the work in fifth grade. She thinks you are ready to move on. How would you feel about coming into my room with the older children?"

Peter was delighted. I'd like that very much, Mr. Fisher."

"Then it's settled. I'll see you here in the morning."

Peter was happiest when he was at school. Mr. Scroggins was curt and demanding when he was home, but Mrs. Scroggins tried to make life as easy for him as she could. He did his chores before going to school in the morning. But before he did his afternoon chores Mrs. Scroggins insisted that he be allowed to sit down at the green and white checked oilcloth covered breakfast table and have a snack of gingerbread and hot cocoa, or some other treat.

Clem Scroggins snarled his objection. "The boy don't need a snack. He took a lunch, didn't he?"

She persisted. "Peter is a growing boy; he needs a snack when he comes home from school." It seemed to Clem Scroggins that his wife was constantly surprising him with her defiance these days.

Only after Peter's chores were finished was he allowed time to do his homework.

Jason did go back to school as he promised. Some of the boys thought to make sport of him, teasing him about being in class with babies, and about the way he talked. His tormentors soon learned that was a mistake. He was quick with his tongue and quicker with his fists. The day they stole the food out of his lunch pail they learned a lesson they would not soon forget. "All right which one of you sunzebitches took my lunch?"

"We'll tell Mr. Trent on you for cussing," one of the boys crowed.

"You do that, you lowdown thief. I'll tell him you stole me lunch, but first I'll knock your block off." With that he landed his fist on the boys nose. Blood spurted down over his mouth and onto his chin. "Now where is my lunch?"

Mr. Trent, the principal, watching from one of the big windows thought, *I might have to intervene. But only if it gets out of hand; the best way to handle it may be to let them settle it. That boy Jason is smart and has street smarts besides.*

Tommy Thompson came forward. "All right, all right. Here it is, in my pail. It was just a joke. I was going to give it back."

"Oh yeah? Don't do it again," Jason picked up a basketball off the ground and started shooting baskets.

Tommy went to the fountain and washed the blood from his face. Not another word was said about the incident.

The morning was sunny and the air crisp a few mornings later, when Jason sat beside Mr. Woolrige in his Model A Ford coupe on his way to school. They drove through the narrow downtown streets past the Evans Drug Store where they sat at a long counter and had their Saturday lunch. *I like the way Mr. Woodrige seems proud of me when he introduces me to everyone. Makes me feel good when he says, 'I want you to meet my new son, Jason. Things are so different here. I'll wait around a while and see how things go.*

Mr. Woolrige interrupted his thoughts. "How are you liking school, Jason?"

"I like it all right, bettern before. *" This school business may not be so bad after all but I'm not telling him, not 'til I decide if I'll run away.*

Jason and Laura often sat on a large rock at the far edge of the schoolyard, and ate lunch together almost every day. The other boys quickly learned better than to tease him about Laura. "Why don't you come over and play with Mary Anne sometime?" Jason asked Laura. She's just nine, but she has all sorts of dolls and girl stuff to play with. I bet she would let you play her piano."

"I don't have time to play. I have too many chores to do after school."

"Then come on Saturday."

"Saturday is the day we have to clean all the rooms."

"Oh." Jason was sorry to hear that Laura had so much work to do. He was beginning to think he was lucky to have been chosen by the Woolriges. They didn't push him like Mrs. Pucket pushed Laura.

Laura liked school, but it was hard to keep her grades up. She often fell asleep from exhaustion before she finished studying her lessons. Her chores were many. There was the table to set for a half-dozen people or more, helping with the serving of dinner, and washing up afterwards. By the time she finished sweeping the kitchen and dining room floors she was always tired. There was no time in the morning to study; the table had to be set for breakfast, and dishes done before she went to school.

Her only solace was getting to be with Jason at school. She and Jason became fast friends. "Man, I love these fried peach pies," Jason told Laura one day as they sat together eating lunch. Sometimes Mrs. Woolrige fixes raisin pies; they're even better. Does your lady fix good lunches for you?" He had noticed that Laura didn't bring much lunch.

"Mrs. Pucket doesn't fix my lunch. I fix it myself." Laura didn't look happy. He noticed her hands were all chapped and red. He broke his pie in half and handed her a piece, saying, "This is way too much for one person, especially after all them biscuits."

"You're sure?"

"Yes, man I'm full." He rubbed his stomach and groaned, making a show so she wouldn't feel bad to take the pie.

"Do you know where Peter is?" Laura asked.

"No and I don't care." He was still acting the tough guy. It was hard to keep up the tough front when the Woolridges were so good to him. He was slowly getting over the idea that they might be up to something. *I'll play along a little longer and see what happens. I don't want to leave Laura here with that Pucket woman. You never know what might happen with that drunken husband of hers hanging around.* He thought of the abuse he had suffered at the hands of his father when he was on a drinking spree.

He was less inclined to want to run away as time went on. Every Saturday Mr. Woolridge took him to the brick factory where he was foreman. At noon on those days they went to the drug store and sat at the soda fountain, and ate hamburgers and drank a malted milk. He had to admit to himself that he enjoyed those times. *Me Da never took me anywhere with him*, he remembered.

New York was growing dimmer in Jason's memory every day. He did think about his father often, and missed him, but he was glad he didn't have to drag him home from taverns anymore, and it was good not to be hungry and have to steal food.

As late summer turned into fall Laura shivered as she and Jason sat on a cold rock on the windy hill. "I miss my little room over Grosspapa's store. I miss the tinkle of the bells as customers come and go through the door. I even miss the rumble of the elevated overhead just outside my window. I miss Ma and Pa Strassburg, too, but most of all I miss Grosspapa."

Jason removed his jacket and draped it around Laura's shoulders. *Why*

37

doesn't that Pucket woman buy a decent jacket for Laura?"

Laura thanked him, then fell silent, remembering Grosspapa's words, shortly before he died, *"Laura, you'll do well; you're made of good stuff, don't forget that. I've set aside some money for your education. Ralph will see to it."* She wondered why Ralph had not mentioned the money before he sent her off to the Children's Aid Society. He must have forgotten. *I promised Grosspapa I would be good and work hard, and that is what I am doing. I will not cry. I'll write Ralph a letter tonight and ask about the money.*

Laura didn't remember her parents. Her grandfather had been reluctant to talk about them. He just told her they were dead. "Leaving you, Laura, is the hardest part about dying," he told her as he languished in bed.

After clearing the supper table after the boardinghouse guests went up to their rooms Laura sat down at her tiny desk and wrote a note to Ralph.

Dear Ralph,

I'm sure it is an oversight, but you didn't mention the money Grosspapa left for me. Please send it to me in care of Mrs. Clare Pucket, 705 Main Street, Weldon, TX.

Yours truly,
Laura Krueger

One rainy morning in mid-November, Mr. Trent called Jason to his desk. "Jason, your work in all subjects has improved tremendously. I think it's time we tried you in fifth grade. What do you think? Think you can handle it?"

"Yes sir, I'm sure I can."

Noting the happiness in Jason's voice he continued. "If we see that you can handle fifth grade with ease, perhaps by mid-term we can try you in sixth. You will be caught up with the others your age."

"I thank you Mr. Fisher and I'll do me best."

"That's another thing, Jason: how about watching your grammar? You know, get into the habit of saying *my*, instead of *me* when speaking of possessions or a relative, and *am not* or *aren't* instead of *ain't*; things like that. Going into higher grades you really need to make an effort. Not that all the students here speak correctly, but I know you can do it."

"Yes sir, I'll try."

Chapter Six
Thanksgiving

The afternoon before Thanksgiving Mrs. Scroggins noticed that Peter looked sad. He sat with his left elbow propped on the kitchen table, his forehead resting in his upturned palm. He held a pencil in his right hand, but it was not moving. He stared at the tablet in front of him. "Peter, is there something you would like to talk to me about?"

"It's just that I miss Sister Mary Katherine. I miss her and Father Kelly. I miss my friends at The Home too."

The next morning when Peter came down to breakfast there was a box next to his plate. In it he found paper, envelopes and six, two-cent stamps. "Oh good, now I can write Sister a letter. Thank you Mrs. Scroggins." *I can write her a letter once a month for six whole months*, he thought.

She looked at him and smiled, "Peter, you have been with us such a short time, but long enough for me to know I love you very much. I want you to be happy. I hope some day you will feel like calling me Mom or Mother."

Peter thought about the words she had spoken: "I love you". Not even Sister had said those words to him. He was overcome with a feeling of affection for this lady who was kind to him, and constantly trying to protect him from the harshness of Mr. Scroggins actions. He reached out his arms to her. "I love you too, Mom. I'm sorry I have no Thanksgiving present for you."

Embracing him she knew she loved him. "That hug is the best Thanksgiving present I could receive, Peter. Happy Thanksgiving to you, son."

Peter was happy at that moment. The other Train Children were often in his thoughts. He hoped they had found good homes. He especially wondered about Amanda.

When Peter went up to bed he sat down at his desk and took out a sheet of the paper Mom Scroggins had given him.

Dear Sister Mary Katherine,
*   Today Mom Scroggins gave me a box of paper and envelopes, and some stamps.*

I'm so happy that now I can write to you, and I hope you will write to me. Mom Scroggins is very good to me.

I wish you could see this place. It's very different from New York. There isn't much concrete here. The streets are paved with red bricks. There are no tall buildings in the town where I live. We have horses, cows and chickens.

The wind howls here a lot, blowing sand everywhere.

Sister Mary Katherine, thank you for giving me my grandfather's watch. I wonder why I was in The Home if I had a grandfather who loved me.

I miss you and all the children, and I miss Father Kelly.

I love you,

Peter

Marie and Elmer Brown tried to find Peter for Amanda. Elmer called Marie aside when he returned from his quest to find Peter. "As I found before, Miss Adams, the caseworker who brought the children here on the train, will not be back for three more months, when she comes to check on the welfare of the children. Mrs. Waters has the list, of course, but she will not return from California until after the New Year." I've asked our friends, some of the parents of Train Riders, and inquired at the police station, but I was unable to locate anyone who had a list of the Train Riders and their prospective adoptive parents."

That evening Elmer was still worried. "Try not to worry, Elmer and come to bed," Marie begged him.

"I'll be up as soon a I bank these coals," he said, as he covered the last embers of fire with ashes in preparation for the night." He continued. " But we must find Peter. Guess I'll have to find another way."

"You will, Elmer, the good Lord willing. I know you will."

The morning after Thanksgiving Elmer sat facing Amanda across the breakfast table. She had asked for Peter again the night before. "Amanda, I tried but I can't find Peter. No, no, don't cry, little one. I have an idea. We'll put a notice in the Weldon Texan newspaper, announcing a Christmas party for all Train Riders in this area. Surely Peter will come to the party. What do you think of that?"

Amanda smiled, showing her little white teeth. Her dark ringlets bobbed up and down as she bounced in her chair and clapped her hands together.

Later Elmer worried, "What if this doesn't work out? It will be worse than before if she gets her hopes up and Peter doesn't come to the party."

"We'll just have to hope for the best. Surely whoever took him will see that he gets to the celebration. He must not have been selected by anyone living in town or we would surely have heard something about him by now."

"We'll not only post the notice in the paper, we'll send notices to all the area schools," Marie said. "Did you see how her big brown eyes lit up when you mentioned that she might get to see Peter? We just have to see that she isn't disappointed. Poor little thing still thinks her folks are alive and will be coming back to The Home to get her."

Chapter Seven

The Invitation

Sam Woolridge set a steaming cup of coffee on Grace's bedside table along with the newspaper. He came from one of those genteel southern families where, often, if there were no servants in the house, the husband brought coffee to bed for his wife. She looked up from the paper. "What a wonderful idea, a party for all the Train Children. Jason will be pleased."

"I wouldn't count on him acting pleased," Sam said. Grace handed Sam the paper. The notice read:

NOTICE TO ALL PARENTS
OF TRAIN RIDERS

Come one, come all—Train Riders and their parents—
to a GALA CHRISTMAS CELEBRATION...
to be held in the Elks Hall,
6 P.M., December 21, 1929.
Bring your favorite holiday dessert.
Santa will be present with a bag of gifts for the children.

Just then Jason passed the door to their bedroom on his way to the bathroom. "Come in here, son. I want to tell you something."

Jason walked back and stood silently in the doorway. As always he was amazed to see Mr. Woolridge take coffee in to Mrs. Woolridge in the morning. He had a blurred memory of a man yelling at a woman, "Get out of that bed and cook me some breakfast." *Was me Da talking to me ma?* He wasn't sure. He remembered the woman had beautiful red hair. *Yes*, he reasoned, *that was me ma. What happened to her? Did she die?* There were times when he hated even the memory of his father, and then other times he longed to see him.

"What?" Jason asked in a sullen voice. This was one of the days he wasn't feeling so good about the way things were going. He had nightmares the night before. He dreamed he was back on the streets of New York City, trying to steal enough food to quell the hunger pains. Those dreams always left him in a bad mood. *They are still being nice all right, but how long will it be before Mr. Woolridge starts cuffing me like me da done,* he asked himself.

"Son, some of the parents are having a Christmas party at your school for all the Train Children in the area. Won't it be fun to see all the children you met on the train?"

"I ain't going to no party to see a bunch of dumb kids. I'd like to go, but I don't feel like tryin' to be nice today," he pouted.

"We don't have to decide right now." Sam said. He was beginning to understand Jason's moods. After Jason walked away he said to Grace, "Now don't worry. He's just testing us again. He wants to go."

Grace poured cream into her coffee and stirred. "I sure hope you are right."

Meanwhile across town Mrs. Pucket sat at her dining room table getting ready for breakfast. She picked up the weekly paper and opened it. The first thing she saw was the announcement about the party. She grumbled to herself, "Well, if that doesn't beat all. You might know some busybody would think of a fool thing like that. That means if Laura goes she'll not be able to serve dinner and do clean-up that night. And they expect me to be present as well. We'll just have to see about that." *If that idiot drunkard I married didn't drink up all the profits from this place I could hire enough help so the girl and I wouldn't have to work so hard,* her thoughts whirled around in her head. She laid the paper beside her plate, opened to the page where the announcement could be seen. She'd see if Laura noticed it.

When Laura stood beside her with a plate of hot biscuits her mood changed; she mellowed. *She's a good girl, smart too, and never a sassy word.* "I suppose you'll want to go to this Christmas party," she said, pointing to the paper.

Laura looked down and read the announcement. "Yes'em, I'd like to go, but, but…."

"We'll have to see what we can do about a dress, and slippers too. Lord, I don't know where the money will come from. And I think we'll see what we can do about getting you one of those new Permanent Wave things. You have beautiful blonde hair, but it could use a little wave." *Clearest blue eyes I've ever seen, her German heritage I guess.*

"That's OK, Mrs. Pucket. I don't have to go."

"Yes, you will go. I can't have the people in this town saying I am not doing my duty by you." She just couldn't admit that she was beginning to feel affection for the girl. She scolded herself; *I loved that lout loafing upstairs in bed and look where that got me.*

Laura was overjoyed. She smiled. "Thank you, Mrs. Pucket. It'll be such fun."

"Laura, how would you feel about calling me 'Aunt'? Something like that? Mrs. Pucket sounds so formal."

"I would like that Aunt Clare."

"That's nice. Now go get ready for school." She was adamant with herself. *I'll have it out with Roy. He will either straighten up or get out. I'll give him a choice. He'll not be spending every extra cent we have for whisky and running around, gambling and Lord only knows what else. I'll see that Laura has a decent life; that she will be prepared to meet the world, and that she will not be so easy to sway as I was when I believed he would quit drinking if only he had someone to love him. Oh, the years I've wasted.* She rested her elbows on the table, cradled her head in her hands and wept.

Laura dressed in her new, tan, long-waisted, pongee dress, donned her navy blue cardigan sweater, and swung her book satchel over her shoulder. She hummed a tune, delighted with the talk she had earlier with aunt Clare. She paused midway downstairs when she heard loud voices coming from the dining room. Aunt Clare's voice was shrill with anger. "You've overdrawn our bank account again. I'm tired of borrowing money from the bank to pay the bills. You know what this means; I told you before that if it happened again I would ask you to leave. I mean it. I want you to pack your clothes and get out of here."

"You don't mean that, baby."

Mrs. Pucket picked up a dinner plate and sailed it past his head. "Does that tell you anything? I may not miss the next time. The circus is in town. I suggest you leave with it. Maybe that *tattooed lady* you are so fond of will take you with her."

Laura creeped quietly down the remainder of the stairs and out the front door. *I wish Ralph would send my money, so I could help Aunt Clare. I'll write him another letter tonight.*

That afternoon when she came home from school there was a brown Gladstone bag on the front porch. She almost collided with Mr. Pucket as he stumbled out the door.

"Shur fault this is happening, you little snivel. All I hear out of her is 'Got to have money to hire more help; can't expect Laura to work so hard'." He picked up the bag and ambled off down the street toward where the circus was parked.

Laura hurried upstairs to write her letter.

Dear Ralph,

I'm serious about needing my money. You know Grosspapa left that money for my keep and schooling. Mrs. Pucket has been appointed my guardian and she will see that I use the money properly.

I'll be expecting it soon.
Yours truly,
Laura Kruger

When Clem Scroggins saw the notice of the party he scowled. "That's a bunch of horse manure. Don't let the boy see this paper, Annie. No use to upset him 'cause he can't go to no party. It's too durn far into town and besides he has his chores to do."

Annie didn't know how, but she knew she had to get Peter to that party. "I think we will be expected to see that he has some sort of social life." She was determined not to let Peter be treated like Billy had been treated. *If I had stood up to Clem then would I have lost my Billy? He was only fifteen years old when I saw him last. He was all dirty and sweaty from a hard day in the field. Will I ever see him again? Peter will go to the party.* That night she tossed in her bed, thinking about what to do. Finally she came to a decision. She slept.

The following morning Annie Scroggins told Clem, "I'll be taking the cream and eggs into town today."

"I'll not have you driving into town today, it's coming up a cloud, and besides you'll let them cheat you. You can't figure in your head."

"I think I can figure well enough to know what I should get for twelve dozen eggs and four quarts of cream. You can take the milk later if you like, but I'll be taking the eggs and cream." She had a plan.

He was surprised at her unwavering tone. "You can't drive them mules. You know how wild they are. They'll run away with you."

"I'll take Chock and the buggy." She remembered how she used to enjoy going to her sewing circle and Woman Society meetings in town. She had been so proud to drive Chock; her young, beautiful blaze faced sorrel, into town hitched to her shiny new buggy. It was a wedding present from Clem. That was back when Chock was a young, beautiful horse. Through the years she had given up her organizations and friends just to keep peace in the family.

"That old horse and buggy hasn't been used for years. You'll get stuck halfway there and me and the boy will have to take off from work to come and get you. We have to get the rest of that hay in the barn before the rains come. You can't do it."

"I didn't ask you Clem. I said, I'm taking Chock and the buggy. Peter is going with me. I took Peter to school in the buggy his first day. Remember? I didn't have any trouble that day."

Clem was stunned by the look of defiance on her face and the emotion that smoldered just below the surface causing her voice to be hoarse with emotion. He walked out of the kitchen, slamming the door behind him. In days past that would have sent her into a panic, but today it just made her more determined to see that Peter had a chance to go to the party. *Yes*, she thought. *Billy would probably be here now if I had stood my ground back then.*

She called upstairs to Peter. "Come down to breakfast, Peter. You and I are going into town." She was glad it was Saturday; Peter was not in school. The look of joy on his face as he came bouncing down the stairs made her efforts worthwhile.

"That's great, Mom. Are we going to a movie?"

"First we will take the cream and eggs to the creamery. We will do a little shopping, and after that, if time permits we'll go to lunch and to a movie."

"I can't wait. There's a Hoot Gibson movie playing at the Avalon."

Annie and Peter had a pleasant ride into town. She told him about the party. They talked about what his life was like in the orphanage. He told her about the watch that Sister Mary Katherine gave him. Reminded of the day he left New York, he said, "I've always wondered why I was left in an orphanage if my grandfather loved me like Sister said. I didn't have time to ask her after she gave me the watch. Miss Adams grabbed my shoulder and said, 'Get on the train, now', and Sister walked away. Then I saw that Amanda was starting to run away. By the time I caught her and got her on the train I knew I couldn't catch up with Sister. I'll ask her, now that you gave me stamps and paper so I can write to her."

"I'd let it go for now, Peter." She was afraid he would be hurt if he knew the truth. She supposed there was a reason why he had not been told.

They took the cream and eggs to the creamery. Bright overhead lights hung from the high ceiling, shining down on glistening white walls. Shiny clean cream separators stood on the black and white linoleum covered floor. Next they went to the General Mercantile store. With the money the creamery paid her Mrs. Scroggins bought a new white shirt and a navy and red tie for Peter to wear to the party. She'd have to listen to a barrage of abuse from Clem, but she could take it. They had a lunch of Chicken and Dumplings in the only diner in town.

"Peter," she said. "How would you like to stop by the Woolridges and see that boy, Jason, you speak of?"

"I'd like that."

They stood on the front porch of the Woolridge home and called, "Hello."

A smiling Mrs. Woolridge opened the screen door. She recognized Peter as the boy she had seen leaving with the Scroggins the day of the placing out. She remembered the words of her husband. "There should be a law against a man like Clem Scroggins taking one of these children. I've heard rumors about what happened to the Scroggins boy, and why Annie no longer comes into town to meetings and such."

"Annie," she said. "How nice to see you. Come in."

"Thank you. Grace, this is Peter. He came to us on The Train." Everyone referred to the train that brought the children from the east as 'The Train'.

"I know. Jason speaks of Peter often. He'll be so sorry to have missed his visit. He went to the factory with Sam." After they were seated in the living room, Grace sensed that Annie wanted to say something to her in private. She said, "Peter, would you be kind enough to go to the kitchen and ask Rosemary to give you a glass of milk and some cookies. And tell her I said Mrs. Scroggins and I would like a cup of tea. Just walk through the dining room. There, right through that door." She pointed to an archway through which Peter could see into a room papered with rose and green flowered paper. A buffet with crystal candleholders occupied a place on the far wall, and a large dining table with a centerpiece of green ivy in a large Chinese bowl graced the center of the room.

Peter walked hesitatingly into the kitchen. Rosemary's dark skin was damp with perspiration as she stood at the wood-burning stove, stirring a pot of soup. A white apron covered the front of her black muslin dress. Turning around to face him, she smiled, showing beautiful white teeth. Immediately at ease, he gave her the message. "You just sit right down there at the table while I get you some milk and cookies."

Mrs. Scroggins got to the point at once. "Grace, I have come to ask a favor of you. I feel it is very important for Peter to attend the Christmas party. You know we live so far from town; it'll be hard to bring him in at night in a wagon or buggy. Clem still refuses to buy a car." She didn't want to say that Clem refused to bring the boy in to attend the party.

"You don't even need to ask, Annie. I will have Jason invite Peter to spend the night with him. I know he will be pleased to have him, and Sam and I will too."

"I do appreciate your help, Grace." *Now I'll have to find a way to get Clem to give his approval—not make a fuss.*

Rosemary brought in a tray with two china cups, a pot of tea, and a plate of cookies. "We've missed you at quilting meetings and forty-two parties, Annie."

"I've missed all of you too, Grace, but there's always so much to do out there in the country."

"I know that's true. How is Peter taking to life on the farm?"

"Peter is doing well. He's a real joy to me. Is Jason adjusting to his new surroundings?"

"He has been a bit of a challenge, but we think he's beginning to get accustomed to going to school and to be a little better disciplined there. We see a lot of improvement in his grammar, and his table manners are improving every day. Mary Ann is starting to tolerate him better and he is being nicer to her."

"I can't remember when I have enjoyed a visit so much," Mrs. Scroggins said, as she and Peter prepared to leave. I have missed my friends these past few years."

"You must come again, Annie. We'll be expecting Peter to spend the night with us after the party."

As they climbed in the buggy, Mrs. Scoggins said, "Peter, I fear we won't have time for a movie today, but we'll come into town again soon and I'll be sure we have time for one then."

"That's all right, Mom. I had a good time talking to Rosemary. She is so funny; knows lots of silly jokes. And she told me about her little boy."

Meanwhile, the Pucket Boarding House was alive with plans for the holidays. Everyone was in a festive mood. Laura was excited at the prospect of her upcoming trip to the beauty parlor for the perm. She couldn't believe her good fortune. Clare made an appointment for her with a dressmaker. Her dress was to be made of emerald green velvet. It was to have a large ecru lace collar and cuffs. They ordered her black patent leather slippers from a Sears and Roebuck catalog. "Thank you Aunt Clare. I've never gone to a Christmas party; it'll be such fun.

Clare was pleased to see Laura so happy. *Now I've gone and done it; I've let my heart rule my head again.*

Laura brought a box of Christmas decorations down from an upstairs closet and they set about hanging a green wreath on the front door, and dressing the large Christmas tree that stood in the corner with tinsel, popcorn, and rows of golden garland.

Chapter Eight
The Party

Jason was happy to be with Peter, but he pretended indifference. When asked by Grace Woolridge if he would like Peter to spend the night and go to the party with him, he muttered, "I guess it'll be alright." Nevertheless, he could hardly wait for Peter to arrive. He wanted to tell him all about his new home and about Laura. He told Peter about how hard Laura had to work. "If I was older I'd take her away somewhere."

Time for the party finally arrived. The Elk's hall was decorated with red and green crepe paper, paper lanterns, holly, and mistletoe. A huge Christmas tree stood in one corner, laden with packages of many sizes and shapes. A long table loaded with refreshments flanked one side of the room, under waist high windows. The placing out program had been in operation many years in Weldon, therefore there were many children from miles around, gathered there with their adoptive parents. Some had grown to adulthood and had families of their own.

"Peter, Peter," Amanda called out when she saw him.

Jason said, "There is that kid who you told stories to on the train."

"Yes, yes."

Peter hurried to where Amanda and her new family sat, and patted her shoulder. "How are you Amanda?"

"I'm good. Oh Peter, I'm so happy you are here. Can you come home with us?"

"I can't go home with you now, but I'll come to see you one of these days."

"Oh good. I hope you come before my papa comes to get me." Peter looked at Marie and Elmer Brown. He didn't know what to say. He knew her parents wouldn't be coming for her.

"Tell me where you live and I'll try to come to see you before too long." That seemed to satisfy her for the moment.

"You can play with my puppy when you come. His name is Bow-wow. He's white with brown spots. He'll like you."

Elmer took a card from his pocket and handed it to Peter. "This is our address and phone number. You are welcome anytime, Peter."

"Thank you." Peter took a piece of Christmas candy from his pocket and handed it to Amanda. He felt sick to know that she was still expecting her parents to come for her. *Why did that hateful Father O'Gorman have to send her away?* He remembered the conversation he overheard the day before they were put on the train when Sister Mary Katherine said they should wait. She thought Amanda's father would be coming for her when he had a chance, but Father O'Gorman wouldn't listen.

Jason walked across the room where he found Laura waiting in line for punch. "See Laura, I told you Peter would be here. He's over there talking to that little girl that he took care of on the train."

"Oh, that's Amanda. I want to see her too." With that she went with Jason to join Peter.

Marie and Elmer Brown were happy to see Amanda's reaction when she saw Laura. She clapped her hands together and called out, "Laura, Laura." They gave their permission for Laura to take Amanda to look at the Christmas tree. The two boys went along as well.

Amanda giggled with excitement as she looked at the shiny garland and tinsel on the tree. Reaching out she gently touched an angel ornament. "My mamma used to call me her little angel."

Laura was to do a reading at this time. She sat on a small chair beside the tree, and taking Amanda on her lap she read in a clear, firm voice. "It was the night before Christmas…."

Miss Harris, the local music teacher, played the piano and led the group in singing Christmas carols. Then everyone was invited to refreshments.

Most of the children had not seen Santa before. They clapped their hands and laughed when he appeared with a pack filled with goodies on his back. Besides stockings filled with fruit, nuts and candy the children received gifts from the Weldon merchants. They gave roller skates to the older boys, little red wagons for the younger boys, dresser sets consisting of hand mirror, hair brush and comb, for the older girls, dolls and china tea services for the younger girls.

Sam Woolridge noticed that Peter didn't get a gift from his new parents. He quietly took from his pocket the watch his employer had given him that day at the company Christmas party. It was still wrapped in Christmas paper. He removed the card with his name and the name of his employer on it. He quickly jotted Peter's name on it, and slipped it under the tree. Santa found it just in time to call out Peter's name.

"Elmer, it is so wonderful to see Amanda so happy," Marie said. "We must keep in touch with Peter and the others she is familiar with. I've heard that Jason boy was a problem for the Woolridges' at first, but he's getting better with their gentle care. However, I'm worried about Laura. They say Clare works her very hard in that boarding house. Maybe we should keep an eye on her, just see how things are going there. I hear that husband of Clare's is a drinker and not to be trusted." They didn't know Clare had sent him packing.

"My dear Marie, you can't save the world or all the children in it."

"I know, but I hate to think of one of these Orphan Train children being mistreated. They are at the mercy of the people they have been placed with."

"I know, but Clare Pucket is a decent woman. I don't think she will let anything dangerous happen to Laura. Now don't worry."

In the first week of the new year Mrs. Waters walked into the bank. She was conservatively dressed in a black wool suit with a mandarin collar. She wore the same large hat with the ostrich feather that she wore the day of the placing out. She walked briskly up to Mr. Knight's office door, knocked and impatiently waited for permission to enter. She was greeted warmly by Mr. Knight. "It's nice to see you back Mrs. Waters." Then remembering that she had gone to California to be with her ill mother, he asked, "How is your mother, Mrs. Waters? I heard she took a turn for the worse about a month ago."

"She did, but she's much better now; that's why I was able to come home earlier than expected. I'm eager to hear what kind of report Miss Adams gave on how the children are doing in their new homes."

"I have not seen or heard from Miss Adams since the day of the placing out."

"What? She was supposed to come back here before Christmas to check on the children. There are a couple of them that I'm particularly concerned about."

"Which two are you talking about?"

"The boy the Scroggins took and the girl Mrs. Pucket took home with her."

"May I ask why the concern about those two?" Mr. Knight asked, knowing all the time the two to which she was referring.

"Oh please, Mr. Knight. You know as well as I do that Scroggins should not have been approved nor should Clare Pucket, seeing that her husband is such a disreputable character. You do know they didn't check ahead with us to get an approved list, this time. I just don't understand it."

"I see what you mean, but I don't know anything we can do about it until she comes back. However, you can rest easy about Clare's husband; I hear he is no longer in town; left with the circus."

"Well, that's good news. "I'm going to go right over to the telegraph office and wire that outfit in New York and see what the problem is with them." That is what she did. She received no answer.

Finally, after spring had come and gone Miss Adams bounced into town in all the latest New York fashion. "And how are all our little cherubs doing, Mrs. Waters?" she asked in her soprano voice when they met for a conference.

"I'm sure I don't know, Miss Adams. My only duty was to see that things went smoothly the day of the placing out, and to keep accurate records of where and with whom the children were placed."

"Well, I'm sure the good people of this town are doing well by their charges, aren't you?"

"I told you when you were here that those children should never have been sent here without prior approval of the foster parents. Furthermore, I told you I was concerned about the appropriateness of a couple of them to take children."

"I saw nothing wrong any of the prospective foster parents, but if it will make you feel better I want you to know that I will visit all of them while I am here."

"You should have been here three months ago. I understand that the first year after the children are placed you are to look in on them at least four times."

"My dear Mrs. Waters, there is no hard and fast rule on that."

"Well there should be."

They exchanged a few more unpleasant words before Miss Adams took her leave. She first visited the homes of the four placed last summer. At the Scroggins ranch she liked the way Mrs. Scroggins and Peter interacted. Jason acted sullen while she was there at Woolriges; her only concern was if they would keep him. They assured her that she was not to worry about that.

When Mrs. Pucket heard that Miss Adams was in town she was so glad she had shooed Roy out of town. She might have lost Laura, of whom she had become very fond, if he had been loitering around. In looking around Miss Adams deducted that the Puckets had taken Laura to help with work in the boarding house, but that was to be expected, she reasoned. She gave them a good mark.

Then there was Amanda. Amanda had a temper tantrum while she was talking to the Browns, yelling, "I want to go home. I want my mamma and papa." She marveled at the patience the Browns had with the child.

The next two days she went to all the homes in the vicinity where children had been placed in the past few years. Satisfied that all was well she left town on the afternoon train the third day after her arrival. *That Mrs. Waters is a hellcat. I'll have to watch my step with her around.*

The lives of the four: Peter, Jason, Laura, and Amanda were intertwined the next few years, and as normal as could be expected for Train Children. The three older ones excelled academically, participated in sports and other activities.

After Peter graduated elementary school he rode the school bus into town and was in high school with Laura and Jason. His life wasn't easy, but Annie saw that he went to school functions and was allowed time to participate in the debate team, and play in the marching band.

By then Jason had caught up with others his age and was in the same grade as Peter. As he gained self-esteem it became obvious he was a natural leader. He was captain of the football team as well as giving Peter competition on the debating team. Time passed quickly those next four years.

Laura remembered her grandfather's words. "You be a good, brave girl, and I'll see you in heaven someday." She displayed self-confidence and courage in everything she did, and was admired by teachers and students alike. She played on the newly formed girl's basketball team and joined the drama club.

Amanda was still plagued with bouts of depression and given to temper tantrums, but under the constant care of the Browns she made average grades in school. It helped that she had a beautiful singing voice; she was successful in school plays. She continued to worship Peter and depend on him for solace and advice.

Chapter Nine
The Growing-up Years

There were happy times and sad times for Amanda. She could be sweet and charming, then minutes or hours later go into a deep, dark depression and wail, "Everybody is lying to me. I know my papa is living." As time passed the fits of rage she occasionally suffered became less frequent. She finally accepted the fact that her parents would not be coming for her, and was more content, but still insisted she was not an orphan. The Browns were pleased with the change in her, but knew her happiness was not complete. Even when she played with other children there was a sadness about her that broke Marie's heart to see. Her brunette hair and almost black eyes told them that; with their Nordic blonde hair and blue eyes, they looked very different than her mother and father. Marie said, "No wonder she feels lost with us at times. There is a constant undertow of deep emotion there that worries me."

Elmer was concerned about that too, but didn't want Marie to worry, so said nothing. Finally, by the time she was ready for high school she quit speaking of her mother and father, but silently determined that one day she would locate them or at least find out what happened to them. She still had moody spells and sometimes would not come down from her room for meals, but most of the time she seemed fairly happy.

In the meantime Peter remained a big brother figure to her. He often had long talks with her when she cried. She said she didn't have girl friends her own age in school. "The boys are nice, but the girls don't like me. I don't know why, I try to be nice to everybody. They still snicker and call me Train Girl. Lou Ellen sits behind me in class and pulls at my hair. When I look around she looks off and pretends she doesn't know what I'm talking about when I ask her to quit, or she says something hateful like, 'Oh, are you afraid you'll loose one of your pretty ringlets'."

Peter knew the way the girls at school treated her was not the only reason for her tears. He also knew that her mood swings put the other girls off, even if they had wanted to befriend her. "Don't let it bother you, Mandy," Peter tried to console her. "I'm sure they like you, they are just teasing."

"I didn't mind so much as long as Mary Anne was here. She was always nice to me; ate lunch with me and talked to me, but I'll miss her now that she is going away to college."

"Jason's sister?"

Yes, Jason' sister, Mary Anne."

"Mary Anne is a nice girl. That's not surprising considering how nice her parents are. They brought Jason out of his pugnacious attitude. He's growing up to be quite a nice young man." Peter was wise beyond his years.

After several such conversations with Amanda, Peter looked at her dark beauty and said, "Now listen, Mandy, I'll be going away to college soon, and I want you to promise me you will not let those petty, jealous girls upset you. I'm sure they'll come around in time, and if they don't, don't be unhappy. You'll be going off to college one of these days; you'll make new friends there.

"Jealous? Why would they be jealous of me?"

"You have beauty, you're a smart girl, and you have a beautiful singing voice. Didn't you get the lead part in your school play last year? It's only natural."

"What will I do without you, Peter?"

"You'll be fine, Mandy."

Peter was the catalyst that held the little group together through the years: Jason, Laura, Amanda, and himself. Soon each of them would be going their separate ways. He worried about Amanda.

Clem Scroggins became ill in the fall of Peter's senior year in high school. It started with shortness of breath and chest pains. A few months later he was hospitalized. Peter and Annie walked along the long antiseptic corridor. "I'll wait here for you, Mom." People walked past him as he sat on a bench and waited. Some of them walked with a cane in one hand while holding the back of their hospital gown closed in back with the other. Others sat in wheelchairs, being pushed around by a nurse. Still others were smartly dressed, there, he guessed, to visit family or friends. Peter was surprised when Annie came to him where he waited for her outside Mr. Scroggins hospital room. "Peter, Clem wants to see you. Will you please go in and talk to him?"

Peter breathed deeply, and smiled. "Of course." He mustn't let Mom see the dread he felt in his heart. *Why does he want to see me? What will he say?* He patted Annie's back, squared his shoulders and walked into the room.

As Clem Scroggins struggled for breath in his hospital bed, he said, "Peter, you have been a good boy and a good helper; never any slack jaw even when

I was hard on you. I want to thank you, and ask a favor of you."

Peter was surprised and relieved; he had not known what to expect. He stood looking down at the large, helpless man. His craggy skin was weather worn from long days under the unrelenting Texas sun. It looked like brown leather against the snow-white sheets. Thoughts whirled around in Peter's head. *He could have been worse; he was gruff and a harsh taskmaster at times, but not once did he raise a hand to me. Some of the Train children have been severely abused.* He nodded is head.

"Will you take care of Annie and help her find her son? I always meant to try to find him for her, but I've waited too late." *So Billy was Mom's son; I always wondered.*

Annie looked on as Peter took the arthritic, callused hands in his and answered, "I'll try." He watched as Clem Scroggins closed his eyes and drew his last breath. He had said his good-byes to Annie earlier that morning.

Annie and Peter bowed their heads. Annie softly murmured a prayer asking God to hold Clem in his loving arms, forgive him for his sins. "Dear Lord, have mercy and smile on Clem. Pardon his wrongs, and forgive him for his sins. And please understand, Lord, that Clem was a good man. His hateful ways were due to an uncontrollable jealously; jealously over a son who wasn't his, a son he was expected to raise as his own, a son whom he found wanting in all the ways that mattered to him. And forgive me, Father for the injustice I did this man, one of your children." She softly kissed Clem's cheek and walked from the room. Two days later he was laid to rest alongside his mother and father in a family plot atop a hillside on the family ranch.

"Peter, please drive me to the cemetery in town." He stood beside her as she looked down at a large granite headstone, wiping away tears. It read:

Robert Williams 1895–1916

Killed in the line of duty to his country

Peter heard her murmur, "Our boy is coming home, dear." She turned and walked silently to the waiting car.

One week after the funeral they sat in the living room, she reading the Weldon Texan and he reading a book explaining the stock market crash of '29. She laid her paper down and sighed. Peter sensed that something was weighing heavy on her mind. *She's worrying about her son.* "Mom, soon after I came here you said something that I have always thought about. I've wondered what you meant when you told Mr. Scroggins that you would not allow him to treat me as he treated someone else. Were you speaking of your son?"

She sat in silence, head down, fingering lace on a handkerchief she held in her lap. "If you don't want to talk about it that's all right, but I did promise Mr. Scroggins I would try to find your son for you. You want me to do that, don't you?"

"I know where he is, Peter. I've known since a short while after he left. He is with my father in Missouri. He has written letters with my father's return address on the envelope all these years. Clem couldn't read, so there was no worry that he would know where the letters came from, and he never bothered with the mail. Billy, my son, asked that I not tell Clem where he was. I didn't. I don't know if that was right. I think Clem suffered from guilt ever since Billy left. I think now that I should have told him; I shouldn't have let him die wondering what happened to Billy."

"Do you want to tell me about it?"

"Come in the kitchen, Peter." They walked across the dining room and sat at the kitchen table where they always went when they had something important to discuss. She placed a cup of coffee in front of Peter and poured one for herself. As she stirred cream and sugar into the dark brew she began to talk. "I was teaching school here when I met Billy's father. He was killed in France in 1916, just days after arriving in Europe. Billy was born two weeks later. After a year passed Clem started courting me. I thought he would be a good husband and father. It was partly my fault that he turned sour on the world. I never pretended to love him as I did Billy's father. I just couldn't. So you see, what I did to him was not fair. I was selfish, looking only for a home for my son and me. Billy was a shy boy; he loved music and books. He wasn't rugged like Clem. Clem was always after him to work harder. He thought reading was a waste of time. He'd speak harshly to Billy. 'Put that book down and get at your chores,' he'd bellow oftener than not. Then one day, after a long day in the meadow, bailing hay, Billy just walked away and he never returned. He wandered around for a couple of months. Imagine at thirteen years old out there in the world on his own. That was about six months before you came to us. I didn't know if he was dead or alive those first two months after he left. A few months before we went into town and brought you home with us, my father wrote to say that Billy had appeared at his door that morning, ragged and hungry."

"Then what happened?"

"He has been with my father all these years. Dad is a math professor at Missouri State University. He provided for Billy's college."

"Why didn't you leave, go to Missouri to be with your father and son?"

"I felt that I had wronged Clem by marrying him, knowing I didn't love him. I did respect him at first, but even that vanished after a while. But I felt I owed him something; I stayed. I knew Billy was safe with Dad."

The year after Peter came to them Mrs. Scroggins started depositing all the egg and cream money she could spare into an account for his education. "Please don't send a statement for this account, Mr. Knight, and please don't mention it to Clem." Mr. Knight smiled and nodded his agreement. She didn't have to tell him why. He understood. He knew Clem Scroggins.

Later that day Mrs. Scroggins said to Peter, "By the time you graduate, Peter, there will be enough money saved for a Junior College education for you."

Sister Mary Katherine kept in touch with Peter, writing at least once a month through the years. Her letters, filled with encouragement, had sustained him during the years he had worked hard to keep up his grades and do the work Mr. Scroggins expected him to do on the ranch. On graduation day Peter walked down the long lane to the mailbox. There was a letter from Sister Mary Katherine. He took the letter from the envelope and to his surprise a check fell out. In the letter she told him the check was to cover four years at Notre Dame. It's money your grandfather left for you," she wrote. *There is that grandfather again; no! I don't believe it. Someday I'll ask Sister, again, who he was and why he put me in the orphanage.* Peter was surprised when he read Sister's letter and he was curious about his grandfather, but he was glad he would not need to use the money Mom Scroggins had scrimped and saved for his education.

Looking forward to Notre Dame was a dream come true to Peter. *Now I will be able to learn more about my Catholic religion.* There was no Catholic Church in this small town. The Scroggins had taken him to their Lutheran church. *No doubt*, Peter thought. *That was the reason Sister Mary Katherine had sent the money, to assure that he go to Notre Dame and learn more about the religion he was born into.* He wondered again, what it meant when she told him, the day he was put on the Orphan Train, that the watch was from his grandfather and that his grandfather loved him. He still wondered why he was in an orphanage if that was true. In answer to his questions her letter said only, "Be patient, Peter, you will understand someday. In the meantime just know that I love you and miss you, and look forward to the day I will to see you again."

Chapter Ten

The Homecoming

Mrs. Scroggens looked forward to Billy's homecoming with double anticipation; her father was coming for a visit too. He had not visited while Clem was living. Peter was a little apprehensive at the news. He wondered how Billy would feel about him, how he would feel about the boy who has taken his place for the last eight years, a boy he had never met.

The day they were to arrive Annie could hardly get her cooking done for running through the dining room and living room on her way to the front porch, looking to see if Billy and his Grandfather were coming up the lane. Finally she said, "Peter, if I am ever to get dinner ready you will have to sit on the porch and call me when you see them coming."

"Wouldn't it be better if I helped you in the kitchen?"

"No, please just watch and let me know if you see them."

Billy and his grandfather came roaring up the lane, a cloud of dust trailing behind them. They arrived in a shiny new, gray Chevrolet about 1 o'clock in the afternoon. It was exactly three weeks after Mr. Scroggins died.

"Mom, Mom," Peter called out.

Annie came running out, her arms open wide. She hugged first Billy, then her father. There was not a dry eye among the three of them. Peter had a hard time keeping tears at bay. Seeing Mom so happy gave him a wonderful feeling.

The occasion was celebrated with an intimate dinner for the four of them. "We'll have a party and invite friends and relatives a little later, " Annie said. The table in the large country style dining room was decorated with fresh cut flowers atop the white cloth-covered table. Peter had helped Annie hang crepe paper in Billy's favorite color. It was draped from the old-fashioned pie safe on one side of the room up to the plain white light-globe that topped the kerosene lamp that hung from the ceiling, and over to the buffet on the other side, forming a canopy of red. "We won't be able to use the lamp while the paper is up there; it could start a fire, but I'll leave it there until after we have our noon meal. I want it to look festive for Billy and Papa," Annie said while they worked.

Billy rubbed his hands together when he looked at the food-laden table. He put his arms around his mother and hugged her tight. "Mom, you've fixed all my favorite foods. Smell that fried chicken, and look at that chocolate pie. Pa's housekeeper is a good cook, but not as good as my mom."

Peter watched this display. *Yeah, it's gonna be all right. As long as he makes Mom happy I can deal with him, good or bad.* He asked, "How was the drive from Missouri, Professor Wilson?"

"It was a long, tiring drive, but we enjoyed the scenery, and we're happy to be back in Texas with you and Annie. Peter, my other grandchildren call me Pa and from what I hear from my daughter here, you're one of the family."

"Thank you, sir, Pa it is. I feel like one of the family." He noticed Billy looking askance at him. *I guess that's a natural reaction,* Peter thought. "Billy, how did you like A & M?" Billy had been in and out of the state two years, but had not felt that he could visit his mother.

"I liked it very much. Now, let's not hear any of those dumb Aggie jokes," Billy chuckled.

In the meantime a few miles away in Weldon, Jason was preparing for a different kind of career. "I know, Pop, you're disappointed that I'm choosing not to go to college. Well see, it's like this. You and Mom have done enough for me, and it's time I went out on my own."

To which Sam replied, "Son, I can't say we're happy you're choosing the Army Air Corps over college, but I know you've made up your mind. You'll make good wherever you are, but we want you to know, we are here for you no matter what."

"I know that," Jason said. "You've always been here for me, ever since that day I stood on that train station platform wondering what was going to happen to me. I planned to run away first chance I had, maybe join a gang. Until that time I didn't know anything except trying to get along on the streets of New York City. I didn't tell you before, but me Da was a drunk. I don't remember much about me Ma. I do remember that she had beautiful red hair like Mom's." Jason fell easily back into his old Irish brogue when he spoke of his life in New York City.

Sam put his arm around Jason's shoulder. "Son, I'm sorry your first few years of life were so hard. We didn't know what happened to make it necessary for you to be placed on the train, but we knew some misfortune had befallen you. We didn't ask because we thought you'd tell us when you were ready."

Jason remembered how patient Sam had been with him during those first few years. "I know I was a bad actor at first. I thought you would turn mean like me Da. I couldn't believe people could be so nice to a strange kid. I thought you were up to something. I know I wasn't nice to Mary Anne, either. I guess I was jealous that she had real parents who loved her and took care of her. She didn't have to go out and steal apples, or anything else, to eat. That's why I wound up in The Home. Officer O'Malley caught me stealing an apple. He told me Da that I would go to a home for bad boys if he didn't take me to The Home so Father O'Gorman could straighten me out. Father O'Gorman's idea of straightening me out was with a strap and a hard thump on the head anytime he had an excuse."

"I admit, son, that a few times in the beginning Mary Anne suggested that we send you back, but Grace and I never even considered it, and after a while Mary Anne loved you just as we did and enjoyed having a big brother. That day at the train station, we took one look at you and knew you were the boy we wanted. When Grace saw your red hair she was a goner. She said, 'get on up there, Sam, and get that boy with hair the color of mine.' She would have been heartsick if someone else had taken you home with them. We've always been proud of you, Jason, and we understood when you got off the track. After all, you were in a strange place with strange people."

"Me Da was mean only when he was drunk, but that was most of the time. Many nights Officer O'Malley would knock on our door and tell me to go to the tavern and get me Da. He used to say, 'He's down there causing a ruckus, if you don't get him out of there I'll have to run him in.' I'd go in and pull on him and beg him to come home with me. Most of the time he would, but he'd be mean and cuff my ears."

"Don't think too bad of him, son. Maybe he had troubles you didn't understand."

"Yeah, he had trouble, all right, trouble staying out of taverns. I didn't know it at the time, but it's a good thing Officer O'Malley made him send me to The Home.

"I'm sure Officer O'Malley thought you would be better off there. He probably didn't even know about the orphan trains. I think they kept that pretty quiet."

Jason said, "I know some of the Orphan Train kids haven't had it so good, but I lucked out, and I appreciate being your son."

"It's been our pleasure all the way and will continue to be so." Sam's eyes brimmed with tears.

That night Sam and Grace Woolridge were awake into the night. "Sam, I hope we are doing the right thing by not insisting that Jason go to college. I'm real worried we might get into war. You know what is happening in Europe."

Sam answered, "Jason is an independent kid. We've always known he had a restless nature. He knows what he wants to do and I think he would resent too much interference in his plans. If we do get into another war it'll be better that he has some training under his belt before it starts. He'll be better prepared and have a better chance to choose what he wants to do."

"I can't help worrying."

"I know. Jason opened up today and told me about his father and some of what he remembers about his mother, which is very little. He said she had beautiful red hair like yours. I'll tell you all about it in the morning. Try to get some sleep, honey. Good night."

A few days later Jason was catching the train to Scott Field in Southern Illinois. The Browns were there to see him off as were Amanda, Peter, and Laura. Peter noticed that tears spilled from Laura's eyes as she waved goodbye. She turned her head away from the crowd and he heard a sob escape her.

Laura and Clare grew very close during the years before her graduation from high school. When Clare's husband, Roy, left town with the tattooed lady, things went much smoother for them. "Good riddance," Clare said to Laura. "Now that he won't be here to spend every extra penny we can hire more help." Her disposition changed dramatically. She made life as easy for Laura as she could. They often had time to talk while hired help cleaned the dining room and kitchen after dinner. Clare told Laura how she met her husband. "He was a handsome musician, a man about town type. He came here with a band out of Abilene to play for a special New Year's Eve celebration. I was smitten with him and he with me, or so I thought. He stayed on and we were married the following week. As time passed he became more and more dependent upon liquor. He said he had no family, nowhere to go. I could no longer support the two of us on my salary. Luckily my parents had left this large house to me, and I started taking in boarders. I couldn't depend on help from him; I had to quit my job at the library. That's where my life was when you came to me. I knew I was working you too hard, but I just couldn't do all the work that had to be done around here. I hope you will forgive me. I'll try to make it up to you."

Laura, being an intuitive child, had sensed that Clare's nerves were taut from the beginning. Now she understood why. She swallowed hard, but couldn't speak; she hugged Clare and kissed her cheek.

Clare said, "I had an easy life before I married Roy. I was an only child, and my folks doted on me. I just didn't know how to handle the situation I found myself in with Roy. Don't ever let that happen to you, Laura; always be strong and take care of yourself. If you make a mistake have the courage to correct it right away. I should have sent him packing as soon as I realized what he was really like."

While Laura and Clare got to know each other better during the months that followed Roy's departure, Laura told Clare about her grandfather and what he said about the money for her schooling, how he had thought his nephew would take care of her. Clare said, "Don't worry about it. We'll manage. When you are older you can confront him and see that you get what is yours. In the meantime just concentrate on getting good grades and enjoy your young years."

After graduating high school the three of them: Peter, Laura and Jason, went their separate ways. Peter went north to Notre Dame, and Jason went into the Air Corps. Laura was all Clare had now and Clare was all Laura had. Clare scrimped and saved to send Laura to Commerce State Teachers' College. Amanda started high school that year.

When Laura came home that first summer she found Jason was home on leave. She missed him when they were apart but went to great pains not to show it.

When Peter was home for summer vacation he helped out on the ranch. The three of them went to movies and played miniature golf. Sometimes the tree of them, Peter, Jason and Laura, took Amanda and Mary Anne along with them. Amanda was getting more grownup and beautiful all the time.

It was obvious to Laura and Jason that Amanda worshiped Peter and was totally smitten with him. Peter didn't seem to notice.

Chapter Eleven
Laura in New York

Four years after graduating high school, Laura sat on a plane headed for New York City. She thought about that first Christmas party; the first time all the Train Children had been together after arriving in Weldon. That was the night she had seen through Jason's bravado; saw that it was a defense mechanism to insure against being hurt, but she couldn't have put it into words at that time. She understood his problem, and from that time on Jason became her devoted best friend; then through the years she slowly fell in love with him. The years in between had been hard at times, but there had been good times as well. Her love for Jason was always there, silently waiting, hoping. Through the years they exchanged letters, phone-calls and he sent her pictures in his snappy air force uniform, but nothing was said of love. She felt restless. Upon graduating college she told Clare she wanted to go to New York. She was livid when she thought about her grandfather's words: "I have put aside money for your schooling. Ralph will see that you get it at the proper time." She had learned something from a lawyer friend of Clare's about how to go about getting the money from Ralph. She needed it to complete her education, to obtain her masters degree, and she wanted to do something nice for Aunt Clare; maybe take her on a vacation; she needed a rest. As she made plans to go to New York City to confront Ralph she thought about Jason and wished the time for his leave had been more certain. She didn't want to miss his homecoming, but felt it essential that she get her business with Ralph settled once and for all. Her letters to him had gone unanswered. She went to New York with Clare's blessing.

"So be careful in the big city, honey," Clare admonished her as she waited for the train that would take her to Abiline to board a train for New York City. Call me. I'll be anxious to hear from you."

"I will. Thank you, Aunt Clare. Take care of yourself while I'm away. And thank you for being my beloved Aunt Clare, not by blood but by action and love." She kissed Clare's cheek and held her close for a minute. "I'll see you soon."

The train ride to New York was uneventful, long and tiring, but Laura was not bored. She brought along a good book and she had so much to think about, so many questions she wanted answers to. Why had her grandfather been reluctant to speak about her parents? Why had he always changed the subject when she asked about them? Why did he trust that thieving nephew, Ralph, to look after her? She needed to find the answers for peace of mind.

When she arrived in New York City she shivered in the coolness of the early spring morning. I s*hould have thought about the difference in temperature; have to get out my sweater when I open my bag.* She took a taxi directly to her old neighborhood. It looked shabbier than she remembered; small buildings in bad need of repair, trash everywhere. Still, the sights and sounds, and the sweet smell emanating from the neighborhood bakery took her back to the days she had spent there as a child.

She heard the familiar tinkle of the bell as she entered what had been her grandfather's store. She looked around. *Now the store is cousin Ralph's; everything looks different, strange, and unfriendly. It's not well kept like Grosspapa left it twelve years ago.* She thought about how arrogant Ralph had been not to honor her existence all these years; his ignoring her letters. Walking in with an air of authority, she looked straight into the eyes of her grandfather's nephew, Ralph, and without preliminaries, asked, "What happened to the money Grosspapa left for my schooling?"

Ralph looked as if he had seen a ghost. "Well, well—I, I. Who are you to come into my store and ask such a question?"

"You know very well who I am. I repeat, what happened to the money my grandfather left for my care and my schooling?"

Ralph placed his forefinger between his collar and neck, turned his neck around to one side as if his neck was itching. "Since you must know, the store fell on hard times. Maybe you don't remember, but we have been through a deep depression. I had to use that money to keep it going."

"This is 1940, Ralph. The country has been coming out of the depression for some while now. Anyway, the money was not left to keep the store open, but for my keep and schooling."

"You don't look like you have gone hungry."

"That is not the point, Ralph. The store fell on hard times? I don't believe it. When Grosspapa was living this was a neighborhood store where people came from all over the neighborhood to shop and enjoy camaraderie with their friends. If that isn't happening now it's because of the slipshod way you are running the store, or your superior manner. Judging from what I am seeing now

I would guess both."

"You know nothing about it. And don't get any ideas. It was all perfectly legal. Your grandfather made me your guardian, and stipulated in his will that I was to use the money as needed."

"As needed for my care and schooling. You didn't fulfill your obligation on either count. You know your being my guardian depended upon you taking care of me, but instead you shipped me off to the Children's Aid Society the day after Grosspapa's funeral."

"Listen to me Missy, and listen good. I was the best choice the old man had. It was for sure that sorry mother of yours wouldn't take care of you. I don't know what he told you about her, but she was a class act all right; he never admitted it, of course. He couldn't bring himself to acknowledge that his spoiled, papered daughter cared more for position and money than she did for her own daughter."

'My mother is dead."

"Believe it if you want to, Missy, but I'm telling you the truth. Your mother is very much alive and living the high life in a brownstone just off Park Avenue. Of course you will not be able to find her by Elsa, her real name. When she left here she started calling herself Lydia. Lydia Worthington is the name she goes by now."

"You are lying. I tell you, my parents are dead."

Laura felt faint. She didn't want to believe what he was saying, but she had always felt there was some shameful secret her grandfather was keeping from her about her parents. "You are just trying to justify taking everything my grandfather left to me. And what of my father? Who is he and where is he?"

"Who knows."

Ralph thought to throw her off, get her thinking about something else. "Are you so sure I'm lying? I can see you are not, but if you insist on thinking so let's see how you feel when I tell you who your mother is and where you can find her. You'll have a way to go, way up to 86th Street, just off of Park Avenue; that's right, 86th Street, off Park Avenue. I know because I know who she took up with when she left here. I see her name in the Society Section of "The Times" once in a while."

Laura didn't know where 86th Street was, but she knew from what he was saying and his attitude that it must be a fancy address. "You're bluffing."

"You know I'm not. Why don't you pay her a visit? See if she will acknowledge that the not-so-stylish girl with a southern drawl is her daughter."

"I beg your pardon, my drawl is Texas, not Southern, and my way of speaking is stylish enough to suit the people I care about."

"No matter. She'll detect right away that you are from some foreign place and laugh in your face at the idea that you think she is your mother."

The thought of her mother being alive did distract her, but it didn't deter her from her goal; that of getting at least part of what was due her. "You can tell all the lies you can think of, but I will have my money."

"Lies, huh? Just go to that address and find out for yourself. And just try to get the money, lady, and see how far you get."

She squinted, looking through slits in her eyes, looking as vicious as she could. "I will, but don't worry, I won't take the store, although I could. I know what I'm talking about, buster. I've consulted a lawyer. So you better come up with the money, plus interest. Do you hear me Ralph? I know now that it's a good thing you sent me away; no telling what would have happened to me if I had lived here with you, unscrupulous and undependable as you are. I can't imagine how you connived to get Grosspapa to leave the store in your care. I know you convinced him that you would take care of me or he wouldn't have made you my guardian." The years she had spent thinking about the injustice fueled her rage.

Ralph squirmed, pretending to be cleaning the counter. She could see he was beginning to worry. "You have no right to come here demanding money after all these years. I could have sold the store and gone to Germany, you know." *She couldn't have touched me there; the money would have been safe.* "You can't take all the money I've saved for my retirement. You're bluffing anyway."

"Try me."

"All right, all right. I'll see that you get the money, but first I want you to check out what I told you about your mother. You'll see who's been lying."

He wants to hurt me by having me see my mother. "I will check it out. In the meantime you get the money together, and see that you don't try to cheat me; otherwise I'll forget what I said about not taking the store, plus the profit from it for the past ten years. See that you don't forget the interest."

She thought about Clare and how she had taught her to be tough, to take care of herself. *Aunt Clare would be proud of me.*

Laura sat studying a city map at the lunch counter in the neighborhood diner. She decided on the Roast Pork and Sauerkraut Special. She looked up to see a familiar face coming out of the kitchen, looking at her curiously. "How nice to see you are still here, Ma Strassberger."

"Laura." Mrs. Strassberger looked surprised. "I thought that was you, but wasn't sure until you spoke. Where in the world have you been child? We were all disappointed when Ralph sent you away to that fancy school for girls without letting us say goodbye. We kept looking for you to come home for holidays, but finally gave up. Your grandfather was such a good man. We never got a chance to tell you how sorry we were about his illness and death."

Laura asked, "Is Papa Strassberger here?"

"He passed away two years ago. He would be so pleased to know you are here and that you are well."

"I'm so sorry. I wish I could have come back sooner. I would have loved to see him again." Laura rose from the booth and put her arms around the elderly woman. After they hugged and both shed a few tears, Laura explained. "My departure was very sudden. Ralph didn't send me to a school for girls. I wanted to tell all of you goodbye, but Ralph rushed to have the Children's Aid Society pick me up the day after Grosspapa's funeral. Fancy girls' school, he told you, huh? So that's why he rushed me off. He didn't want Grosspapa's friends to know the truth, that he was shipping me off to be rid of me."

"Oh you poor child. That awful man. If we had only known we would have loved to have you live with us. You know we have no children of our own, and we always loved you from the time you were a little tike."

"I loved you and Pa Strasberger too."

"Your grandfather always brought you in to eat. You loved our specialty, roast pork and sauerkraut with boiled potatoes.

"I remember. I'll have the same today. To answer your question about where I've been; two days after the Children's Aid Society took me in I was put on a train with forty-five other children, most of them orphans, and sent west to Texas."

"Oh, no, Child."

"It's all right, Ma Strassberger. There I was given over to a Mrs. Pucket, a woman I call Aunt Clare. I've come back to see about some money left to me by Grosspapa. Ralph tells me my mother is alive. I'm going to look for her."

"Oh, dear, I wouldn't do that. Let sleeping dogs lie, I always say." *I don't want Laura to be hurt by what she will find if she finds her mother.*

"Thank you for your concern, but don't worry, I can take whatever I find. I've learned to be strong living with Aunt Clare. It was hard at first, but after we got to know and understand each other we got on fine. I've come to love her and I know that no matter what happens here I will survive intact. She sacrificed to send me to teachers' college, and now I want to collect the money Grosspapa left for my schooling. I want to do something nice for Aunt Clare, and use some of it for graduate school."

"Still, honey, I'd just leave well enough alone. Get your money from Ralph and go about your business. Forget what Ralph said about your mother being alive."

"I know you are trying to protect me, but I must know the truth. Please don't worry about me; if my mother rejects me I won't be crushed. I'll still have Aunt Clare, and now you."

"You dear, sweet girl. I wish we had known what was happening. Mr. Strassburger and I would not have allowed you to be sent away. We would have made such a fuss that Ralph would have had to let us have you."

"My life has been fine, but I do appreciate that, Ma Strassburger. I'll come back to see you before I leave New York. I've never forgotten you and Pa Strassburger. You were always kind to Grosspapa and me. We looked forward to taking meals here."

Laura returned to her hotel room. *Glad I could find an affordable room here, not far from the old neighborhood.*

The next morning Laura dressed in her best suit, brushed her light blonde hair into a becoming pageboy, and took special care with her makeup; a natural colored foundation, a pale brushing of rouge and light lipstick. She tried to look as sophisticated as she could. Then she made her way to the closest subway station. With the name and address Ralph had given her in her hand, she started on the miserable journey to look for her mother. *What will I find? Will she be happy to see me? I'll soon know.*

Laura alighted from the subway at Lexington and 59th Street. She knew she could go to a subway station closer to 86th Street, but she wanted to walk through Central Park. *I need to relax; get myself settled before I meet this woman who Ralph says is my mother, this Mrs. Henry Worthington.*

On 5th Avenue she walked past the Metropolitan, wishing she had time to go in. While walking through the park she saw children playing. Others were being pushed in carriages, some older ones skipped along beside their mothers or nannies, stopping to pick up sticks or leaves. *That's the kind of life I would have had, I suppose, if my mother had loved me and kept me with her.* When she reached Park Avenue she turned left, then left on 86th Street. As she walked up the steps to the imposing apartment building where Ralph said her mother lived she almost lost her courage. *Remember Aunt Clare's words: be strong.* She squared her shoulders and approached the doorman. "I'm here to keep my appointment with Mrs. Henry Worthington. She is expecting me." She hated to lie, but knew that was the only way she could get past this man. She expected to be asked her name and maybe even quizzed about the nature of the appointment. She had a story all ready, but luckily she didn't have to use it.

"Certainly ma'am. Step into the elevator." He whisked her up to the eighth floor.

"Oh dear, I've forgotten the apartment number."

"Straight ahead, ma'am."

A maid in a black dress and white apron and cap answered the door. Laura thought a little sarcastically, *What? No butler?* A smirky grin played briefly on her face. She was hurt to think that her mother had lived in this luxury all these years while aunt Clare struggled to care for her. *I will not cry.*

"Madam is waiting for you in her boudoir, down the hall, second door on the left." *Oh, so the doorman knew Mrs. Worthington was expecting someone,* she thought. *That's why he let me in without a hassle.*

Laura walked into the room and held out her hand. Ignoring the offer of a handshake Mrs. Worthington said, "Did you bring the swatches?"

"I have no swatches, Mrs. Worthington." She looked at a well-groomed, pampered-looking woman.

She was haughty in her reply. "No swatches? Don't waste my time. You may as well go and don't come back without swatches for me to choose from."

Laura had rehearsed this scene many times in her mind. "Mrs. Worthington, my name is Laura Krueger." She waited for the name to register with the stranger before her. It did. The woman turned very pale. She said nothing.

"I'm your daughter."

The woman hesitated. "You are mistaken. I have no daughter."

Laura looked at her trembling mother. *How could she be my mother?* However, she knew it was true. Her resemblance to this woman was remarkable.

"Sorry, my mistake." She turned to leave.

"Wait, wait. Since you are here please sit down. I'll ring for tea. You can tell me why you think I am your mother."

At least the woman is curious enough to want to talk to me. That has to mean that in her selfish, shallow way she must be interested in knowing something about me, and must have loved me at one time. "Are you sure you want me to stay?"

"Yes, please." In a shaky voice she asked, "Where do you live? I don't believe that is a New York accent."

"I live in Texas. I was sent there by the Children's Aid Society when my grandfather Krueger died. Grosspapa gave me his name. I'm not sure what my father's name was or is. I'm happy with Grosspapa's name. He was wonderful to me."

The woman's dark blue eyes became glossy with unshed tears. "When did your grandfather die?"

"Twelve years ago. He left his nephew Ralph in charge of me. Ralph couldn't wait to be rid of me. He called the Children's Aid Society the day after the funeral, and asked them to come for me. He told them I had no home and no one to look after me, never mentioning that he was my legal guardian. He was interested only in Grosspapa's money. Three days later I was on an Orphan Train headed west. A woman named Clare Pucket took me into her home in Weldon, a small town in the West Texas Panhandle."

"I'm so sorry, my dear." She sat quietly for a minute. Laura stood to leave. "Please don't go. Here is our tea now." She waited for the maid to leave the room after placing the tea tray on an octagon-shaped cherry table beside her chair. "Since I have no children and you have no mother, perhaps we could stay in touch. I could be sort of a mother figure to you. I could explain it to my husband in that way. And please, Laura, call me Lydia." She poured their tea as she talked, avoiding Laura's eyes.

Laura pondered this request. *She is not going to recognize me as her daughter, but wants to be my friend? She knows that I know she is my mother, but she can't admit it. It would be very awkward, and in fact impossible now, to admit to her husband and friends that she has a daughter, perhaps born out of wedlock, a daughter she was willing to abandon for riches.*

"Tell me about yourself. Have you had a good life?"

"It was hard at first, but it has been better the past few years. Aunt Clare scraped the bottom of the barrel to send me to college. I plan to teach school. I'll be going back to school this fall to work on my masters. That's one reason I came to New York at this time, to make Ralph give me the money Grosspapa left for my schooling."

"You don't have to ask this Ralph for money for school. You don't even have to see him. My husband is a philanthropist. He will be happy to pay for your graduate school. We have no children of our own. Please let me help you."

Laura thought, *So she doesn't want me to see Ralph. She's afraid I'll learn more about her.* "I have already seen Ralph. He told me how to find you."

"Well, I don't know what that depraved man told you, but I have no children."

71

I should enjoy turning the screws on this woman, but how can I when she stands before me a weak, shaken woman. Besides it was not Laura's nature to be mean. She reached out and took the quivering, outstretched hand. "I'm sorry to have bothered you. I hoped to find my mother here."

The woman looked down at her feet; a slight whimper escaped lips.

"Please, Laura. Can't we be friends?"

Laura felt sorry for the woman. "Very well, Lydia." Laura thought, *Some people are just weak, others just selfish. Which is my mother? Perhaps both.*

"Let's keep in touch," Lydia begged. "Will you write and let me know how you are doing?"

Laura answered, "Yes, if you like. She took a notepad from her bag, wrote her name and address on it, and handed it to Lydia." All the time thinking, *why couldn't you have wanted to know how I was doing years ago when I really needed you?* She turned to leave.

The woman stepped between her and the door, took her in her arms and whimpered, "Thank you Laura. You will hear from me soon."

Laura said goodbye to her and left with a sad heart; sad for what might have been.

The following day when she stopped to say goodbye to Mrs. Strassberger she asked her, "Why do you think Grosspapa told me my parents were dead?"

Ma Strassberger answered, "I know he hoped he was doing the right thing. He told us he just couldn't bear to tell you that your mother left you with him when you were only three years old, and never returned. Your mother called him a week after she left and told him she would not be coming back, and not to look for her. I know he didn't feel he had lied. Your mother was as dead to him as your father who was killed in the war. He now lies in Flanders Field in far-away France."

Laura sobbed uncontrollably. The first tears she had shed since she left New York as a child. *I will not cry.* But the unwilled tears flowed.

Chapter Twelve
Jason

In his letters Jason told Laura he was working hard to further his education in the service. By the end of his fourth year he had graduated from Weather School at Chanute Army Air Base as a meteorologist, and had attained the rank of Captain. "I'm so proud of you, Jason," was her constant refrain when he told her of his promotions. He never failed to let her know that he was proud of her accomplishments as well.

The Woolridges were proud of him, too. "That's great, son. The military people recognize leadership qualities when they see them," Sam said to Jason, on one occasion when he called home.

"How's it going Pops and how is little sister?" They were pleased that he now thought of Mary Anne as his little sister. They remembered how he had ignored her and at times was just plain rude and bullish to her when he first came to live with them. They felt good that she would have a big brother to look after her if anything should happen to them. They truly loved him as if he was of their own flesh and blood.

Jason was disappointed when he came home in mid-June to find Laura had already left for New York. Now he was ready to make a commitment if Laura was willing. *Why didn't I tell Laura that I loved her last summer?* He was disappointed and disturbed to find that no one knew how to get in touch with her to let her know he was home; his leave time had been uncertain when he wrote her last. His Mom Woolridge tried to comfort him. "She'll be calling home any day now. You'll see. She told Clare she would be in touch."

"But when? I have only two weeks leave. Mrs. Pucket said she didn't pin her down to a certain time to call. Maybe her mother or father is still living. She said her grandfather was always reluctant to discuss what happened to them. Maybe she'll find one of them and stay there with them. Maybe she'll find them all broken down and sick and stay there to take care of them. Maybe if she doesn't find either one of them she'll be so heartbroken she'll just stay there and keep looking."

Finally, Sam spoke up. "Settle down son. That's enough maybes. Have a little faith in Laura's judgement. She's not going to go there and just disappear."

"I know, Dad. It's just that I love Laura and would be sick if I lost her."

"Have you told her that?"

"Not in so many words, but I'm sure she knows."

Grace said, "Well then, I suggest you tell her at once."

"Just how is she supposed to know?" Sam asked.

"Okay, I intend to tell her as soon as I see her again."

Laura called and spoke with Jason that evening. She was non-committal about what was happening. "I'll tell you all about it when I see you."

"And when will that be?" Jason wanted to know.

"I promised Amanda I would go to the Orphanage and see if I could find out anything about her parents. I'll do that tomorrow. Then the next day I will go back to pick up my money from Ralph, and say my goodbye to Ma Strassberger. I'll get into Abiline Friday around 10:30 in the morning."

"Who is Ma Strassberger?"

"A very dear friend of Grosspapa's and mine when I was a child. I'll tell you about her when I see you."

"Good enough. I'll meet you in Abiline," Jason said. "Please hurry home to me Laura."

"I will hurry home to you, Jason, my dear love."

He was thrilled with that greeting. *I know she knows I love her.*

The next morning, upon entering the large brick building on the hill, Laura thought about how hard it must have been for Peter and Amanda to leave this place of security and go all alone to a strange place with strange people. As she walked down the hall toward what she assumed to be the office, a small nun who looked to be well past middle-aged greeted her. "May I help you dear?"

"Yes, thank you. I'm looking for Sister Mary Katherine."

"You are in luck, I'm Sister Mary Katherine." Her dark eyes twinkled.

"Sister, my name is Laura Krueger. I was on the Orphan Train with Peter Martinelli twelve years ago. We were placed out in the same town. We have remained friends. He told me you might be able to help me locate the parents of Amanda Polletta, a little girl he befriended on the train. She was only seven years old at the time. Do you remember her?"

"Oh yes, I remember little Mandy. She was a beautiful, but sad, little girl. But please, tell me about Peter. I hear from him from time to time, but I worry that he hasn't always told me the true story about his life. I've always felt that he was trying to protect me from knowing the real truth about his situation."

Laura thought for a moment, and thinking that it would serve no purpose to tell the Sister that Peter had had a hard taskmaster in Mr. Scroggins, she said, "Sister, you couldn't wish for a better mother for Peter than Mrs. Scroggins."

Sister looked a little doubtful, but said, "I'm so glad. I didn't want to let Peter go but the priest in charge of The Home at that time insisted. I felt terrible after he went away, but have been grateful that his new family let him keep in touch with me by letter."

"Now about Amanda, Sister?"

"Amanda's mother died shortly after she and Peter were sent west. God forgive Father O'Gorman for what he did to that man. And I, I had promised to keep her safe until he could take her home; I didn't once think that I would not be able to fulfil my promise. It broke my heart that I was not able to keep my word to Mr. Polletta. He was distraught upon learning that she was no longer here. It was so hard to witness his anguish.

"You mustn't fret. From what Peter told me you could not do anything about it."

"Still it bothers me terribly that I couldn't keep a promise that I made."

"Peter has spoken of you in his letters, Laura. You have been a good friend to him. I love you for that."

"Peter has been a good friend to me too, as well as some of the other children who were on the same train we were on. You can be very proud of him."

Sister Mary Katherine looked pleased. She smiled and patted Laura's shoulder. "You know my dear, I am not supposed to give out any information about the children or their parents, but there are times I think God's laws supersede the rules of institutions such as this. As far as I know Amanda's father is alive."

"Can you find it in your heart to tell me how he could be found?"

"I really don't know. He finally gave up trying to find out where Mandy was a few years ago. I'm sure he could be found, but how would it set with her present parents? What would you do if you found her father?"

"I would give the address to Amanda; in a few months she will have her eighteenth birthday. I know Mr. and Mrs. Woolridge would be happy for her to see him, especially if he is the right sort of man."

"He seemed perfectly nice when he was here last. He was crestfallen, of course, because I couldn't tell him where Amanda was; just that she was no longer here. I did assure him that she was well cared for. I knew because Peter had spoken of the wonderful people by whom she was adopted."

"His name is Paul Polletta. Come with me, dear." She went into her office. Laura followed. She pulled out a file drawer. "You know, my dear, these records are confidential. Please excuse me for a few minutes. How do you take your tea?"

"With milk, Sister."

Sister Mary Katherine gave Laura a knowing smile as she left the room, closing the door behind her. Laura wasted no time in finding the name she was looking for. She made a mental note of the last known address of Paul Polletta.

After they enjoyed a cup of tea, Laura said, "I must be on my way, Sister. Thank you for your hospitality." Both of them knew her gratitude was for something more than the tea.

"Good luck to you, my dear. Give Peter my love, and please give him this letter."

She held out a yellowed envelope. "It will explain a lot about so many things and why I was so determined to keep him close to me. I think he knew I was devastated when I had to put him on that train, but the Lord does work in mysterious ways. As it turns out he may have had a more normal life, maybe better suited to meet the world, than if he had stayed here with me."

"Thank you, Sister. I'll give it to him." They embraced and Laura picked up her bag and walked rapidly out the door and down the walkway to the street where she hailed a cab to take her to the address she carried in her head, the address for Paul Polletta.

Chapter Thirteen

Laura's Return

Carrying a dozen long stem American Beauty roses Jason paced back and forth on the platform while he waited for the train to arrive. When the appointed time came and passed he went back inside the depot to inquire about the reason for the delay. He checked with the desk clerk. "Some sort of trouble on the tracks, nothing serious," he was told.

Jason was relieved. *Thank God, no train wreck. Soon Laura will be coming home to me. I can't wait to tell her I love her, but surely she knows.*

One hour after the scheduled arrival time the train came chugging down the tracks. The roses were a little wilted, but a happy Jason ran to place them in the arms of a happy Laura. He didn't have to tell her he loved her. The heartfelt hug and kiss he gave her relayed the message well. "My dear, my dearest Laura," was all he said. The warmth with which she embraced him left no doubt about his love being returned. The drive back to Weldon was a happy one. For their lunch they stopped for a picnic in a park in Weatherford. As they sat on a green, grassy hill, facing a pond, they watched the ducks eat the leftover bread they tossed into the water. It was there that Jason said to her, "Laura, I love you. Will you be my wife?"

"Oh, Jason, yes, yes, yes."

Only two things diminished their joy; Laura had found upon going to the address Sister Mary Katherine gave her, that Amanda's father had died just two years before. Laura said, "I can't tell her Jason, Peter or the Woolriges will have to tell her."

"True, that would be best. I hate to think what will happen when they tell her."

"Another thing, Jason, I know you didn't ask me to look for your father and I hope you don't mind that I did. I checked with the County Clerk's office. I'm sorry, honey, but your father is dead. He died in his sleep five years ago. I'm sure there was no suffering."

"Thank you Laura, and thank you for caring. I've always wondered about him, but just couldn't face going there to see him. You see, after I was with

Mom and Pop for a while I started thinking about my life before I came to them; I remembered something that made me dislike my father more than ever. I won't burden you with the details, but I will just tell you that he was very unkind to my mother. In fact, I'm pretty sure he caused her death by his meanness and drinking. I'm sorry he was like he was, but I can't be too brokenhearted about his demise."

"Oh, Jason, I am sorry. I love you, Jason. I think I always have, even on that first day on the train when you made fun of my hair, asking if they turned a bowl over my head to cut it."

"Did I do that? Sweetheart, I'm sorry I was such a punk. And I'm so glad the Woolriges could see past all that bravado and know that there was a decent, scared kid under there somewhere, and that they had the patience to find him. He reached for her and held her to his breast. We won't let anything spoil our time together tonight. I have to leave by week's end."

She laid her head on his shoulder and thought about how lucky they were to have each other.

Upon returning home, Jason couldn't wait to tell the Woolriges about his engagement to Laura. They were delighted with the news, but not surprised.

Grace hugged Laura. "I'm so happy to welcome you into our family."

Sam shook Jason's hand and congratulated him, and kissed Laura's cheek. Even Mary Anne got in on the act, saying, "Now I'll have a sister of my very own, not just a bruiser of a brother." She gathered both of them in her arms.

Laura was overcome with joy. Tears of happiness swam in her blue eyes. "And now I will have parents and a sister as well as my Aunt Clare. I love you all."

Jason said, "I know Laura is eager to see her Aunt Clare to give her the news. We'll see you later." They took their leave.

Clare was as pleased and excited as the Woolriges' had been. She welcomed both of them with open arms. "Jason, I'm so happy for you both. I know you will take good care of my dear Laura."

Chapter Fourteen
Peter Goes to New York

Peter waited anxiously for news from Sister Mary Katherine. "Laura, did you see Sister?" When she told him she visited The Home and spoke with the Sister, he wanted to know all about her. He was relieved when told that Sister was happy, but sorry to hear that she looked frail.

"And Peter, I have a letter from Sister for you. She said she didn't want to trust it to the mail, but I am concerned about why she asked that I hand it to you instead of waiting until she sees you. I know you've told her you will be seeing her soon. I worry that she may not be well."

Peter took the letter in his hand, looked at it and saw that the envelope was yellowed with age. "She must have written this years ago, Laura. I'll keep it to read in private."

When he got home, in his room, he opened the letter with trembling hands.

My dear Peter,

Today my worst fears have come to pass. I had to let you leave me. My heart breaks. I will pray for your wellbeing every day. I pray that someday I will see you again.

By the time you read this letter you will be a young man. When you are grown up I know you will wonder about your beginnings and why you were placed in The Home. *Please know it was not because you weren't loved. Your precious mother, my younger sister, Rebecca, died in childbirth. Your father was a brave soldier who died in one of the last battles of World War One. His name was Thomas Martenelli. He and Rebecca were not married, but you were conceived in love the night before Thomas left to go overseas. He never knew he had a son. Your mother asked that you carry his name; he was your true father.*

Your grandfather was ill at the time, and begged me to take you to The Home and see that you had a good life. One of his last acts was to give me the watch and ask that I give it to you with his love.

My dear nephew, I hope this news will not disturb you, but instead will give you peace of mind, and let you know where you came from.
I will always love you,
Your Aunt Mary Katherine

With tears clouding his vision Peter opened his valise and gently put the letter inside. He knew what he had to do next. He would go to New York and see his aunt Mary Katherine very soon.

The next morning Peter walked into the barn where Jeff, the hired man, was doing chores. "Jeff, what do you think about Billy? Is he doing a good job with the ranch?"

"I recken he had ranching in mind when he decided to go to Texas A & M. He has buckled down and is taking care of this place. He is very different from Scroggins, but just as efficient, and much easier to work for. Mrs. Scroggins tells me she would like to have you both here, but I think it's real smart of you to go on your way and do something you like to do. You wuz always a good worker, but she knows you wuz never cut out to be a farmer or rancher."

" I hope you are right. I didn't get to know Billy very well. I left for school soon after he and his grandfather came for a visit.

Jeff said, "I know his grandpa spoilt him, knowin' how bad Clem had treated him and all, but he's made of good stuff. He's seeing to things around here real good."

"Thank you Jeff. I feel better hearing you say that. I don't want Mom to have any more heartache."

Peter walked into the kitchen; Annie was putting a pan of biscuits in the oven. She turned around just in time to see Peter as he entered the door. "Umn, there's nothing like the smell of bacon frying and coffee perking at the same time," Peter said. He took the letter from his pocket and handed it to her. "Mom, when you read this letter you'll understand. It answers some of the questions I've had all these years." He didn't trust his voice to stay steady if he read it to her.

As was her usual way, she asked Peter to please sit down, then she set a cup of coffee in front of him. She wiped her hands on her apron, took the letter, and sat down at the table to read it. When she finished she wiped her eyes on the back of her hand. "This explains a lot, Peter. I'm happy for you to finally learn about your family. You know we consider you our family, but I know it's nice for you to find that your beloved Sister Mary Katherine is also an aunt by blood as well."

Then, "Mom, you know I couldn't love you more if you were my flesh and blood mother, but I have to go to New York City before long to see Sister Mary Katherine. I'm worried about her. Laura said she looked frail when she saw her."

Annie Scroggins turned and faced the window for a minute, then with glossy eyes placed the letter back into the envelope and handed it to Peter. The dreaded time had come and she was not ready for it, but pulling herself together she smiled and turned to face him, "Of course, son, I understand. I'm happy you have found out about your beginnings and that Sister Mary Katherine is your aunt, and about your mother, father, and grandfather."

After placing the letter back into his pocket Peter crossed the floor, looked into Annie's sad face and hugged her. "I knew you would understand, Mom. I won't be away long. I have an interview with Mr. Fisher in the morning. He has assured me there will be a place for me on staff next fall. There's an opening for a Math and Chemistry teacher. I'm qualified to teach both."

Annie smiled and breathed a sigh of relief. She had been afraid he meant to go away forever. She hugged him to her bosom. "I would be disappointed if you didn't go to her, Peter. Please tell her for me that I am sorry she couldn't keep you with her, but since that was not possible I am thankful we had the privilege of having you with us."

"Mom, as we have discussed, I'll be taking an apartment near school when it starts, but I'll be around often even after I move into town."

"I understand, but you know you are welcome to live here with Billy and me. Your room will always be here for you."

"I know, but I think it best to live closer in. There'll be a lot of functions to attend at night, games and all. He thought, *Billy should have his mother to himself for a while longer, and Mom should have her son, at least for a while. He'll probably be getting married soon enough.*

That evening Peter answered the phone. Father Murphy told him he should come at once. Sister Mary Katherine was seriously ill. He dreaded to tell Mom he had to leave sooner than he had intended, before Billy got home from visiting his grandfather in Missouri; he didn't want to leave her alone. He needed to talk to someone. Laura. He hadn't seen her since he got home. He could always talk to Laura about anything. He went to the phone and turned the crank. "Hello Central, give me Clare Pucket's house, please." He waited for an answer while watching the door, hoping to complete the call before Mom came in from the garden. "Laura, can you meet me at the Lone Star Café later on this morning?"

Laura was puzzled. "Is something wrong?"

"Let's talk when I see you," he said.

He opened the door and called out, "Mom, I'm going into town. I need to pick up a few things for my trip." He didn't tell her that his plans had changed, that he must leave right away. He'd tell her when his plans were complete.

Laura parked her old Model A coupe in the sparse shade of a mesquite tree and hurried into the restaurant. She rushed to the booth where Peter sat looking at a menu. "You sounded worried, Peter."

"Tell me, Laura, how did Aunt Mary Katherine act when you saw her? Did she appear to be sick?" He loved using the word 'Aunt' instead of Sister. She had always felt like family but, somehow, knowing she was blood kin gave him an inner happiness he had been lacking before. *Of course*, he thought. *Mom felt like family too, but still it felt good to know that he had a real living blood relative.* He prayed she would live long enough for both of them to enjoy the kinship.

"As I told you, Peter, she looked frail, but happy. Why?"

"Father Murphy called last night and said she has leukemia. He said she had been in remission for a while, but became ill again last week. He said he thought I should come there as soon as possible. His exact words were, 'You never know what turn these things will take'."

Laura was thoughtful. "I wonder if that is why she ask me to bring the letter to you. Maybe she was afraid the leukemia would rage out of control before she would get to see you."

"Possibly. Sounds reasonable. Now I understand; she didn't want to take a chance that the letter would get misplaced and I would never know the truth about my mother and father."

"Peter, I have to tell you something I didn't get a chance to tell you last night. I wanted to spend as much time with Jason as I could. He has to leave so soon."

"What's that?"

"I found out that Mandy's parents are both dead. I was waiting for a chance to tell you and ask you to tell her that her father is dead. She'll take it better from you. She has always looked to you for guidance."

"What a shame her father died before she got to see him again. She will be heartbroken. I'll talk to her as soon as I get back, but first I should alert the Browns so they will be prepared to comfort her and handle any problems that may arise. They have been so good to her, but I fear they have spoiled her. I

82

don't know how she will react. I hope they will wait until I can be there when they tell her."

"Peter, I know you will be busy making plans for your trip to New York. Would you like me to tell them? I can run over there when I know she is not home."

"That is good of you, Laura. I would appreciate it very much."

They reminisced about the Orphan Train ride, how scary it had been to leave familiar surroundings and come to this place; so different from what they were accustomed to. "We were the lucky ones, Laura. But I believe things worked out for the best for both of us. Some of the others were less fortunate. At least Mr. Scroggins didn't beat me. I've heard that happened to some of the boys and even worse for some of the girls. Jason was lucky too. The Woolriges are fine people. Amanda has been loved and cared for, but she has not been happy. She has never been convinced that her parents aren't alive and looking for her."

He changed the subject. "I understand Jason is home on leave. I hope I have a good visit with him before I have to leave, but it doesn't look likely to happen."

Laura placed her left hand on the table and wiggled her fingers. Peter's eyes widened as he looked at the diamond on her ring finger. "Hey, congratulations. When did this happen, and why was I not informed?"

"It was all so fast, Peter. Unfortunately he has only a few more days before his leave is up. Had I known when he would be home I would have waited to go to New York. There is no time for a formal announcement. I'm glad I got to tell you myself. You know you've always had a special place in my heart."

"And you in mine. When will the great event take place?"

"Not until I get my masters in elementary education. That will enable me to teach almost anywhere, even overseas when and if Jason is sent over."

"Well, Jason is a lucky man. Thank you for meeting me today, Laura. I needed to talk to you. Keep an eye on Mandy while I'm away." He paid the check. "I'll walk you to your car."

As they walked she took his arm. "Peter, please do be careful in New York. I'll be thinking of you and Sister and hoping for the best. She was very kind to me, I loved her instantly."

"Remember us in your prayers."

"Of course. God bless."

One quick embrace, he opened the car door for her, got in his car and drove away. She watched him go. *The girl who marries Peter will be very lucky.*

Peter stood waiting for the train that would take him to New York. He heard the mournful whistle as it neared Weldon. He heard that sound, the sound he had been so acutely aware of ever since that night long ago when he and the other children made their way into the unknown; would it haunt him forever? Would it always give him an empty feeling in the pit of his stomach, a feeling of aloneness? *Yes, Jason is a lucky man. He has Laura.*

As the train wobbled along on uneven tracks Peter had time to think; time to think what his life may have been like had his mother lived, and if his father had come home from the war. He was happy that his aunt Mary Katherine had sent the letter explaining the facts of his birth. It filled in a part of the puzzle that had been missing.

New York City was confusing to Peter; the tall buildings, the streetcars, and the cluttered streets gave him an uneasy feeling. When he arrived at Mercy Hospital where Sister Mary Katherine was being treated he immediately went to seek out her doctor. "How is she, Doctor?"

"These things are tricky, but right now she is doing very well. She'll be so happy to see you. She has spoken of nothing else since she received your wire saying you were coming."

"Do you have any instructions for me before I go in to see her?"

"Just be yourself. She is eager to see you."

Upon entering the room Peter saw immediately how much she had changed in the last twelve years. Her slight body barely made a hump under the bedcovers, but her eyes still sparkled with life when she raised her arms to enfold him. "My sweet boy. I am so happy to see you. I knew you would come."

"Of course, my dear Aunt, I couldn't wait to see you." He bent to kiss her parched cheek, and then held her fragile, purple veined hands in his as they talked.

"I hope you weren't shocked or displeased when you read the letter."

"On the contrary. I couldn't have been happier. To know about my parents and to know that you are my aunt has made me feel like a whole person; I always felt like something was missing. I want to thank you for all you have done for me, both when I was a child and since I have been grown-up. I want to thank you, too, for giving me Grandfather's watch. I will treasure it always."

"I was so sad when I had to let you leave The Home. I tried my best to keep you here where I could watch out for you, but Father O'Gorman wouldn't hear of it. Of course he didn't know the circumstances of your birth, but I don't think it would have made any difference if he had. Now I'm thinking that your going away may have been best for you. You had a more normal life."

Peter thought, *Not for anything in the world will I have her know the rough times I went through with Mr. Scroggins.* "I missed you Auntie, after I went away, but Mom Scroggins was wonderful to me."

"The word 'Auntie' is music to my ears, darling boy." She closed her eyes and drifted off to sleep, tears-puddled just below his eyes.

As he sat watching her face and thinking how sweet she looked even in her weakened condition the door opened and Father Kelly walked in. "My dear boy, Peter, how are you?"

"Father Kelly, what a nice surprise. I didn't know you were here. I'm so happy to see you." He reached out to shake his hand.

Father Kelly took his hand, pulled him to his chest and put his arms around him. "I wanted to do that when you were a lad; it wasn't permissible to show affection to our charges in those days."

"Father Kelly, I missed you so much after you left. One consolation in having to get on that train was that I knew you went out west, and being a kid I didn't know how big the west was. I imagined that I would find you out there."

"I missed you too, Peter. I missed being here with all the children." He patted Peter's back. "My, my, you have grown into a handsome young fellow. I'm not surprised; you look very much like your father."

"You knew my father?"

"Yes indeed, my boy. We were friends long before I became a priest. In fact we were raised in the same neighborhood. He was a lad in knee pants when I went away as a candidate for the priesthood."

Peter thought, *That explains a lot.* "Father Kelly, I'm so happy you are here to be with Aunt Mary Katherine at this time."

"Aunt Mary Katherine? So you know."

"Yes, she sent a letter that she wrote the day I left here on the Orphan Train."

"I see. I'm retired now, and when Father Murphy called and told me that she was gravely ill I came as quickly as I could. She asked that I give her last rites."

"Oh, Father, is it that near?"

"She is prepared for the unavoidable. Her faith will carry her through. The doctors will make her as comfortable as possible."

Peter visited with her constantly the few days before she died. After the funeral he bid goodbye to Father Kelly and invited him to come to Weldon to visit him.

"You may be surprised one day, my boy. I may do just that. I still live in Arizona."

Peter returned to Weldon with a heavy heart. He was glad he had the opportunity to see his aunt, but sorry they didn't have more time together.

Chapter Fifteen
Peter Returns Home

Amanda was waiting for Peter at the train depot in Weldon. As soon as he stepped off the train she ran to him, clasped her arms tightly around him, and kissed him passionately on the lips. "Hey, hey, what's this?" he asked as he took her hands in his and pulled her arms away from his neck.

"You always act that way, Peter. You treat me like a kid sister. I'm not a kid and I'm not your sister," she pouted.

"No, Mandy, you are not my sister. You are a dear, dear friend of whom I am very fond, but I do feel like I could be your big brother."

"Well, you are not, and I'm not a kid anymore, and I'm sick and tired of you treating me like one. Remember that, Peter," she said as she flounced off and got in the car. She didn't utter a word of sympathy for the passing of his aunt.

"Oh my, what have we here," Peter murmured to himself as he walked inside the depot to pick up his bags. *I fear she is quite spoiled; her thoughts are all about herself: 'me, me, me'. I suppose that is not unusual for a girl her age. However, I am concerned about that amorous kiss.*

Peter slid onto the seat beside Amanda, trying to act lighthearted, as if he had forgotten about the more than sisterly kiss. "What's up kid? Any thing exciting happen while I was away?" He realized his mistake as soon as the word "kid" left his mouth.

"Don't you ever listen, Peter? I just told you I am not a kid, and I'm tired of being treated like one. I'll thank you to remember that and not call me kid again."

"Come, come, Mandy. Knock off the dramatics." He thought to head off any further theatrics, which he fervently hoped was what he was witnessing here. "What's come over you, Mandy? I thought you'd be glad to see me. You haven't even asked about Sister."

"Glad to see you? Glad to see you? You know I'm glad to see you, but I don't care a fig about your trip, and I don't care about Sister Mary Katherine. She let them take me away, didn't she? I know Papa came back for me. Anyway, I know about Sister. I saw Laura in town. She told me your aunt died. You didn't even call to tell me, but you called Laura."

"I'm sorry Amanda, and I'm sorry you are upset. I thought it would be just as well to wait until I got home. It was a very busy time, with the arrangements and all. I knew you would understand."

"You knew wrong. I don't understand."

"I explained to you long ago that Sister tried to keep both of us in The Home, but Father O'Gorman wouldn't let her. Okay, let's have the real reason you are upset. "

"I told you. I'm not a kid and I am not your sister and I'm tired of you treating me that way. I'm not saying it again, now remember that this time. I love you, Peter."

"Mandy, honey, I love you too. You are like the little sister I always wanted."

"I don't want you to love me like a sister, and don't call me honey unless you mean it."

"Honey is a word that can be used for anyone a person is fond of, and you know I am very fond of you."

"Fond? I don't want fond, I want love."

Peter's heart was heavy. Surely he hadn't expected to come home to this.

"Besides, nobody tells me anything," Mandy sulked. Laura has been acting funny. I know she knows something about my folks, but she's not telling me. I thought you would tell me when you got home, but I can see the way you are acting, you don't intend to tell me either."

"Mandy, I know you are anxious about your folks. I'll come home with you tonight and we'll talk about it then. Okay?" Peter wanted her to be with Elmer and Marie when he told her everything.

"I'm worried about what I'll hear about my mother and daddy, but that's not all that's bothering me. I could take the worst news, in fact I'm expecting it about my mother, but I need to know you love me, not as a sister, but as a sweetheart. Do you understand, Peter?"

"I understand, Mandy, but you are upset, and with good reason, worrying about your parents and all." Peter wondered if it would be better to wait until after she got over the shock of finding that both of her parents were dead to talk straight to her concerning his feelings for her. He decided to do it now. "You are one of the most important people in my life Mandy. I've cared for you since that awful day we were shuffled onto that train and told we were going west. I repeat, you are like a little sister to me. I hope you know that you can depend on me as you would an older brother. We are family, you and I.

We are lucky. We have each other, as well as Mom Scroggins and the Browns. And there's Jason and Laura. All of us love you Mandy."

"I don't care about your Mom Scroggins or Jason or Laura. I love you. I always have, and not as a big brother. I think I would have died of fright and loneliness on that train if you hadn't been there drying my tears and telling me stories."

"Now listen to yourself Amanda. First you said you didn't care about Sister Mary Katherine, now you say you don't care about Mom Scroggins or Jason and Laura. Those are people I love, people that I just told you I consider family. You know you love Jason and Laura. Just calm down and think about it. You are mistaking devotion and familial love for romantic love. You know I am devoted to you and I love you, but as I said, like an older brother loves a little sister. After you have had time to think about it you will agree with me."

Amanda turned off the key. "You'll have to drive." She looked at Peter with tears streaking black mascara down her cheeks. She had overdone her makeup, trying to look older when she went to meet him. She opened the car door, got out, slammed it, and walked around to the passenger side and crawled in. "Scoot over." She huddled in the corner of the seat and pouted, refusing to look at Peter.

Peter was filled with dread, thinking what might happen when she was told about her parents. He knew the Browns had been good to her, perhaps too good. They had spoiled her trying to make her happy. It was clear to him now that she always expected to get her way. He dreaded what lay ahead for her.

The Browns expected Peter to come home with Amanda as arranged. They wanted him to be there when they told her the sad truth. "Come in, Peter," Elmer said. "We were sorry to hear about Sister Mary Katherine passing."

Before he had time to answer, Amanda ran past Elmer and Marie and hurried upstairs as fast as her legs would carry her. They knew from the look on her face that something was wrong. "What happened, Peter? Did you tell her about her parents?"

"No. Something else came up."

"What on earth could get her so upset?" Elmer asked.

"I would rather she tell you that. All I can say is that I'm sorry it happened now, just when she has this other bad news to face. Maybe we should wait for another time, a better time, to tell her about her parents."

While they were discussing the best approach to take, Amanda came running down stairs carrying a small bag. "I'm going to New York to find my parents. I've waited long enough. Take me back to the depot, Peter. If you don't take me I'll walk. I'll wait for the next train headed east."

Peter didn't know if she was just having a tantrum, but he couldn't take the chance that she might go. He locked his arms around her waist from behind, and held on to her as she tried to open the door. "Listen to me Mandy. You can't do that."

"Watch me. I'm eighteen years old, I have enough money for a train ticket and nobody can stop me," she screamed. "If you won't take me to the depot I'll walk. I tell you, I'll walk." She struggled with all her might to escape his grasp and get the door open, her face contorted and red with rage.

Elmer loosened Peter's grip on Amanda and enfolded her in his arms. Marie quickly embraced her from the other side, surrounding her so she couldn't run out the door. "My darling little girl," Elmer whispered. "You know we love you, and it hurts us to have to tell you in this way, but there is bad news about your parents." He told her as gently as he could the circumstances of her parent's death. She quit striving to free herself; he felt her go limp, all the strength seemed to seep from her body as she crumpled to the floor.

Marie screamed, "Peter, call doctor Rainey. Quick!"

Peter ran into the hallway where the phone was located on the wall. As he turned the crank he made the sign of the cross with his other hand and prayed, *Dear God, let Doctor Rainey be in.*

"Central, give me Doctor Rainey's home." *It's late. I'm sure he's home by now.*

Marie bathed Amanda's face with cool water. She opened her eyes, but stared straight-ahead, not blinking, saying nothing. Peter tried to talk to her, but she only stared at him. They didn't know if she heard what he was saying to her. Elmer carried her up to her bed. Doctor Rainey arrived a few minutes later and gave her a sedative. Marie explained to him what happened; that Amanda just found out that her parents were both dead, after believing all these years that at least her father was alive. "She tried to tell us from the beginning that she was not an orphan, but we thought it was a child's imagining that what she wanted to believe was true. We have known only two weeks that her father lived until two years ago. We had to tell her tonight. She was threatening to go to New York to find him."

Dr. Rainey said, "We've known all along that she is a fragile, delicate child. It's not surprising that she would react this way. We'll just have to watch her and hope for the best, but with care I feel she will be all right. Let her sleep tonight. She'll feel more like talking in the morning."

Peter thought it best to let the Browns handle the situation for a few days.

He kept track of her progress when he saw one of them in town. Two weeks later when he did go back, Elmer had a long talk with him before he went up to see Amanda. "She told us all about the talk you had with her the night you came home. She told us about being in love with you, and she told us how you told her that you loved her only as a little sister. We should have realized what was going on with her. We knew she idolized you, but we didn't know it was a serious thing, anything but a friendly affection." He hung his head. "We should have known."

"I'm sorry, Mr. Brown, I suppose I should have guessed. You know I'll do anything to make her life happy, anything short of marrying her. I would even consider that if I thought that would really make her happy, but that wouldn't be fair to her, knowing how I feel. In the end she would be miserable."

"I know, son. She'll come around. In fact I think she's already beginning to understand that maybe her feelings for you are sisterly worship for an older brother; one who has been wonderful to her, and perhaps she realizes a little puppy love was thrown in."

Peter was relieved. "You don't know how good that makes me feel. I do hope you are right."

"We have spent countless hours talking to her, not only about her feelings for you, but about her folks as well. We've tried to assure her that we understand how she feels, and God knows we do, but there is nothing we can do now."

Peter asked, "May I go up to see her?"

As he stood outside her door he heard her phonograph playing, *"What do they do on a rainy night in Rio."*

Great. She can't be too unhappy, singing along with that happy song. He knocked lightly on the door.

"Come in Peter. I heard you drive up in that rattle-trap you call a car."

Ah, good sign, she's ready with a quip.

Upon entering the room he saw that she was propped up in bed with a book in front of her. "I'm glad to see you're feeling better, ready with the wisecracks."

"What do you care how I feel, Peter?"

"You know I care." He was careful not to call her "kid" or "honey". "You know how sorry I am that your parents passed away. Try to see it this way: I'm sure they were happy that you weren't there; they didn't have to worry about you contracting tuberculosis. You know your father died of the same disease. They knew that if you lived there with them you would have stood a real chance of getting it too."

"I know that. Peter, I'm sorry I made such a fuss the night you came home from New York. And I'm sorry for what I said about not caring about Sister Mary Katherine, and you know I do care about Jason and Laura. I know it's not fair to Mother and Daddy for me to carry on like that; they've cared for me all these years, but I was worried about what I was going to hear about my parents."

"It's okay, Mandy. I understand. You were feeling lost and alone. You don't ever have to worry about being alone as long as I live. I have a deep affection for you. You are my friend, my best friend."

"I'll be okay, Peter."

He smiled. "Now you're talking." He tousled her hair. "I see you got over the big love of your life in a hurry."

"I didn't say I was over it. I'm just working on it. And I'll thank you not to mention it again, you clod. Mother and Daddy may be right. They explained to me that big brothers are always around, even if husbands disappear."

"That's my girl. The little sister I've always wanted." He chuckled, feeling free to gently tease her now.

"Peter, be serious. I was hurt, but I know I'm lucky to have you for a friend. And I'm lucky to have Mother and Daddy. I wish, of course, that I could have seen my father again, that he could have known that I was being cared for. And I'm not happy about the way I was shipped off out here and people told that I was an orphan, but I know it can't be helped now. I'll just have to live with it and make the most of what I have."

"Mandy, your father did come back for you after your mother died. He did know that you were being cared for. You know I wrote to Sister all these years. I told her about the Browns and how much they loved and cared for you. She said your father was happy to know that."

"Thank you Peter; that makes me feel better: just to know that he knew I was alright."

"I'm so happy to hear you say that, Mandy. As I've told you before, Sister Mary Katherine tried to keep you at The Home, but the priest at The Home at the time would not hear of it. She tried to keep me there too. I heard the conversation from outside the hall door where I was hiding."

"Thank you for telling me that, Peter."

As Peter was saying his good-byes, Amanda said, "When will I see you again?"

"Oh, I don't know; before too long I'll have to beat you in a game of bowling."

"That'll be the day. I beat you three games in a row the last time."

"It's impolite to brag, Miss Mandy." He was so pleased to hear her joke.

Chapter Sixteen

Peter Finds Love

Peter felt good as he drove to the high school that morning in early September. Now that Amanda's attitude seemed to be improving he could concentrate on getting his schoolroom ready for the first day of school. He was looking forward to teaching and coaching. He parked his car in the teachers' parking lot, took a box of supplies out of the trunk of his car and walked to the front door. Just inside the hallway he met Mary Anne coming out of the principals office. "Mary Anne, what are you doing here? I thought you had gone back to school."

"Peter, how nice to see you. I came down for some last minute advice from Mr. Fisher before heading out tomorrow. He told me he was principal of the grade school you went to when you first came here. He's pleased you will be teaching here this fall."

"I'm happy to have him for a boss man. I'm glad I ran into you, Mary Anne. Can you wait a few minutes while I stash these things in my room? I'd like to chat with you over a cup of coffee or lunch."

"Thank you, Peter. It's a little early for lunch, but I'd love to have coffee and maybe a piece of Mr. Rippy's apple pie."

"I'll meet you back here in a few minutes, soon as I put these things away and speak to Mr. Fisher. If you'll leave your car here I'll bring you back for it."

They rode together to the café. It was an old café, but served the best Blue Plate special in town. Ira, the head cook, was a cousin of the owner. There was a long counter with stools, and across a wide isle a row of booths along the entire length of the building. Peter chose a booth at the back so he and Mary Anne could talk in private. "Their hot apple pie is great with a slice of cheddar slipped under the top crust. Have you tried it that way?"

She answered, "No, but it sounds good."

As they sat waiting for their pie and coffee to be served, Peter asked, "What do you hear from Jason?"

"Good news. He's to be stationed back at Chanute Field in Illinois to be an instructor the Weather School there. Laura has decided to do her graduate work at the University of Illinois. Chanute is only about fifteen or twenty miles from there, so they can get married sooner than they originally planned."

"That's great news. Have they set the date?"

"It'll be sometime in the spring after Jason finds a place to live and gets settled in."

"How is the kid?" Mary Anne asked.

"You mean Amanda? I think she's doing well considering what she has been through. Naturally she had to go through a period of mourning. By the way, she doesn't like to be called 'kid' anymore. I'm trying to watch it."

"I'm sorry. I didn't know it bothered her. I'll be careful not to call her that again."

"I think she is going to be fine now," Peter said. He didn't mention the other disappointment Amanda had had to deal with, finding that he was not in love with her.

"You do know she has a colossal crush on you don't you, Peter?"

"Not anymore." he answered. "She has done a lot of growing up lately in the past month."

As he sat looking at Mary Anne he realized that in her calm way she was beautiful. "Her burnished brown hair, blue eyes and fair skin made a very pleasing picture. He also realized that he was enjoying the conversation immensely. "Would you like to go to dinner and a movie tonight?" He didn't want to rush things, but she would be leaving for the University in Austin the next day, and he was suddenly taken with a desire to know her better. "I'll understand if you have last minute packing to do."

She smiled. "I'm almost finished with packing. What time should I be ready?"

Peter wondered why he had not noticed her lovely mouth before. She had always just been Jason's little sister to him.

After that first date it was understood that every time Mary Anne came home they would go out together. Many Friday nights, when there was no game or meeting he had to attend, Peter headed for Austin. By the time spring came and Jason and Laura's wedding day drew near they had fallen deeply in love.

Upon arriving in Austin one sunny Saturday afternoon in March Peter felt happy. In his pocket he carried a small velvet box. He stopped along the way and dropped a nickel in the slot of a public telephone. "Hello, Mary Anne, I'm just getting into town."

"Oh good. I'm waiting for you. You still want to go for a picnic?"

"Sure, I'm just outside a small restaurant. I'll get a couple of sandwiches and some cold drinks and chips."

"Don't you dare; I've prepared a picnic basket filled with food fit for a king; well, fit for us, anyway."

"I'll be right there. Shall we have our picnic on the banks of the Colorado and watch the sun set?"

"Hubba, hubba!"

"I thought you'd like that."

Peter took a stadium blanket out of the trunk of his blue Ford V8, and spread it on the ground. "There now, my love, a pallet fit for a queen who is about to spread a feast fit for a king."

Mary Anne laughed as she placed the food on a yellow and white Mexican tablecloth she had spread on the ground next to the blanket. "This is a beautiful place, overlooking the ever flowing Colorado River."

The picnic finished and the dishes packed neatly back in the basket, they sat on the blanket holding hands as they watched the moon cast its light on the water.

"Did you ever think of all the beautiful mountains and valleys the water in that river has passed by on its way here to sparkle in the moonlight just for us."

Peter pulled Mary Ann onto his lap. "Hadn't thought about it, but I'm happy it did and happy we are here to admire it."

Taking her in his arms he kissed her ardently; his kiss was returned with like passion.

"My dear Mary Anne, I love you." He took the velvet box from his pocket, opened it and took her hand. Holding a diamond ring ready to slip on her finger. "Will you marry me, Mary Anne?"

"Oh yes, Peter my dear love. I'll marry you."

From a jukebox on the deck of a pleasure boat anchored nearby came the familiar strains of the old favorite, "*Moonlight Becomes You.*"

"The engagement was announced in the Weldon Weekly News. Jason phoned Peter from Scott Field, in Illinois. "I hear you and Mary Anne are engaged. Laura and I have talked and we think a double wedding might be nice. What do you think, fella?"

"Sounds good to me, but don't you want to have a military wedding?"

"No, all of our friends and family are there in Weldon. It's where we fell in love. We'll do it there regardless."

Peter discussed the idea with Mary Anne and she was elated. It was understood that she would finish the remaining two years at the University of Texas; he would continue to teach in Weldon. In the meantime, they would be together as much as possible. All the families involved were delighted with the news of the idea of for a double wedding.

The big day came in June of 1941. The wedding was held in the Lutheran church with many townspeople attending. Amanda looked smashing and radiantly happy as she greeted Peter with a kiss on the cheek. "Congratulations big bro." Then turning she slipped her arm through the arm of her boyfriend, William Russell, one of the town's most eligible young men.

War was already raging in Europe, and the United States was heavily involved in the Lend Lease Program; shipping arms and ammunitions to England. Jason's parents were concerned, thinking that war was likely coming, but prayed and had faith that God would watch over Jason, knowing that he would surely be affected if the United States should become involved.

The End